BLACK GODS
short stories

by
Femi Ojo-Ade

African Heritage Press
San Francisco   Lagos
2002

African Heritage Press

San Francisco   **Lagos**
P.O. Box 170613   23 Unity Road Ikeja
San Francisco   Lagos, Nigeria
CA 94117   Tel:1 -4972044
Phone: 415-469-8676

e-mail: afroheritage9760@aol.com
www.africanheritagepress.com

Library of Congress Catalog number: 2002103634.
OJOADE FEMI

Cover Design: Dapo Ojoade

Selections:2002
Fiction, Literature, African Literature,African American Literature,
multicultural Studies

ISBN: 0-9628864-4-0

For Biodun, Jimi, and Motunde

Contents

To The Reader: Black Gods

The protagonists of the stories in this collection are mostly Africans, privileged Africans, a generation born during and after the Second World War, but suffering no major effects of that "white man's war." We -yes, including you, because you are likely to be part of that generation- were what you may call "privileged outsiders." We grew up with the struggle for independence but never played an active role in that struggle. Any cataclysm that took place seems to have passed over our intelligent, or potentially intelligent, heads. Mark that word; for, intelligence has nothing to do with acquiring a bundle of paper qualifications. Rather, it is the savvy to survive, either as hero, or villain.

A good number of us were raised in an era of government colleges, bourgeois institutions entered by sheer force of chance, but potentially placing us on the highest rung of the social ladder. It was also the era of Western education which, for many of us, meant a trip to the white man's land, the land of milk and *honey* (that is, money), to study especially the sciences -such as, engineering, medicine, biochemistry, geophysics, etc.- even when we were talented artists, linguists, and historians.

Many of us grew up on the fringe of that African culture vaunted by well-known Africans and Afrophiles. We felt, indeed, privileged not to have to undergo the rigor (or disgrace, as we were made to believe) of studying our mother-tongues in the secondary school. Learning the basics of our languages, of our culture, was considered utterly bush and our most revered leaders, in spite of their high-falutin speeches on the political podium, aided and abetted our snobbishness. We were taught mainly by white teachers (another great privilege!), and we often thumbed our noses at those jealous hordes unlucky to be tutored by some "incompetent" brother or sister on the next street.

For those reduced to attending such "second-rate" schools, traveling overseas in itself made a privileged African out of a supposedly second-class citizen.

So, armed with our fledgling bourgeois concepts, we trotted off to the métropoles, and to America, in particular, to seek the golden fleece and to attain the utmost in Civilization. Our bastardized souls fell easy prey to all forms of moral and psychological colonization. Excellent students that we were, we quickly learned to beat the hypocritical, dehumanizing, and materialistic master at his own game. We ended up leaving the best of ourselves abroad while returning home with the worst of the other world. Black gods, that is what we are, thrown out of white heaven into Black Africa, but ready to rule over our kith and kin like true agents of the civilizer.

Irony of ironies: the very people that sent, or saw us off, to the bastions of Civilization, scoff at us when we return with the highly desired golden fleece in our pockets. Our American training is anathema to many an established civil servant back home, or to certain British-oriented professors. Maybe our detractors are jealous of our affected tongues, our civilized demeanor (no, italics wouldn't be necessary anymore), our opinionated carriage, and specialized knowledge. Maybe they never thought that the effects of computerized minds and breathing robots could be so absolute upon the very human souls of their loved ones. Or, maybe they just don't understand! Whatever reason there may be, they have come, in their large numbers, to reject us, and we, them. However, the rejection is coupled with a spontaneous embrace; for, after all, we, too, are sons of the soil, their children, sisters, and brothers. Many of them secretly covet what we have, although they do not know what exactly it is. Meanwhile, we loved, and still love, the conflict and the controversy. Again, a question of privileges. We are black gods, loathed and loved, blessed with the power to possess our people while being prostituted by the oppressor from abroad.

Then, there were the inevitable wars and conflagrations turning our dear continent into a land of infernal chaos. Some of us have participated in them, thank goodness, sharing in the worries and woes, in the death and destruction, in the glory and gains. But many others ran away from it all, privileged bastards that we were, and remain, never interested in staining our soft hands and lily-white suits, forever seeking the solace of our intellectual ivory-towers. Some have profited from the chaos, while supposedly remaining aloof; others have lost their very dear ones while not caring for the conflict. For once, privileges have become shackled, indifference has been punished, sometimes unjustly.

Many of us have obstinately remained outsiders to the evolutionary process of our society. Maybe there is no way to change our perspective. But the confusing events seem to rain upon us with ever-increasing intensity. Maybe we'll be compelled to change. But that would mean forgetting that we are black gods, rigid in our right to absolute stupidity, revered by the peasantry, spited by leaders mired in the mud of materialism and corruption.

We all wallow in some form of emptiness, and sham happiness, and self-gratification. Privileged and unprivileged alike, we are all Africans aspiring to certain things stamped with two words: self-interest, and survival. If you are African, it means living corruption and torture. It means acquiring riches through crookedness. Cash squandered by hare-brained moneybags with no thoughts of tomorrow, or of others. The horror of concealed white domination and deification in these days of Independence and Freedom. It has meant, and it continues to mean for many of us, existing as hybrids, mixing African with English, French, Portuguese, or other foreign languages and cultures, and not knowing which of our glorious cultural entities to keep. For, to start with, many of us don't know what culture is. Like black gods living white lies...

It is with all these facts in mind that you, the reader, part of the privileged few, should read the stories in this collection. As you will quickly confirm, they are not folk-tales or fireside stories. They are far from being "African" in the sense that, in certain hypocritical quarters, what is African supposedly contains a touch of music, dance and songs, a spicing of proverbs and mythology, and a tinge of life in a village untouched by Western ways. But they are African, because they deal directly with the plight of millions of Africa's children at home and abroad, today's victims and victimizers, and tomorrow's leaders and followers.

If blame is to be shared out -and some would call that a dangerous act- we would agree that our generation deserves a large portion of it. Many still prefer to be first in hell than last in heaven. And, yes, the religious symbolism is deliberate, ironical, soothing, and sad. We are dazzled by the glow of the metal, without bothering ourselves to scratch below the surface to assert its quality. We continue our headlong dash into modernism, a highly-touted fad even among those who have never sat down for one second to analyze and understand its connotations and implications. Many of the sufferings of those in exile are unknown to those at home and, to save face, we consistently tell lies. We are lecturing, or studying, at Harvard, Yale, Oxford, Toronto, Sorbonne, wherever, whatever. We are also sweeping streets in Amsterdam, or Paris. We are the greatest cabbies in Washington, D.C., and New York City. We are celebrated crooks in Chicago, and odd-job nonentities in Atlanta, or Houston, or Los Angeles. And, yes, in each of those places, and more, we are among the best and brightest, even if the civilized savages in power refuse to admit it. We are unwanted aliens in Britain. We are harassed overseas and envied and harried by our own people back home. Contradictions weigh down our existence, but we always try to bluff our way through it all. Age, too: all of a sudden, we find that certain people we used to cringe to, prostrate for, respect overzealously, are now our colleagues. That our little nieces and nephews, and children, are almost catching up with us in the mad race for the acquisition of paper-qualifications. That we are losing our hair and are being addressed as brother and uncle by pretty girls whom we would love to give a ride in our foreign cars. After the joy rides and many rendezvous in nameless hotels, the girls become familiar and begin to call us by our first names, a habit that we find almost embarrassing. Our age is telling on us, slowly but surely, and we complain of "these little brats who don't respect their elders". As if a foolish old man deserves anyone's respect! Contradictions. Privileges. Chaos. Like black gods aspiring to white heaven populated by angels clad in black and spitting fire from their coal-tar faces.

And now, talk of our black complex. In Africa. In America. Everywhere. Black solidarity is at the root of black freedom. Solidarity in suffering. Freedom to forget. Solidarity of solitudes. Freedom of fettered souls. And the war continues, for the right to imitate, and self-destruct, both on the continent and in the diaspora.

Dear reader, you may throw down in disgust the book you are about to read, or feel some empathy towards the characters of this fictional world. You may even find yourself somewhere in these stories. Whether your reaction is positive or negative, the act of reading and reacting in itself will be satisfactory to the writer. For too long, many of us have existed without living, as we kept mimicking life, and wallowing in apathy. We never like to tell or face the truth. The characters of these stories, through their acts and speeches, reveal some fundamental truths and, hopefully, you will grasp some of them, and understand. No bliss here, no earthly paradise, no mythical, pastoral tale of laughing men and women with no care in the world. Tragedy is the overall theme; and comedy, too. The objective is to explore the universe of certain human beings, to understand their problems and arouse in you, dear reader, the desire to act in a manner that would alleviate some of the existential difficulties, if not to completely solve them.

You must remember that fact and fiction are inextricably linked; that laughter leads to tears; that happiness is but a stone's throw away from sorrow; that you and I have often laughed to keep from crying, even while we are ignorant of the very reason for crying and laughing, all at once. And, as you close the book, you may rest assured that, sooner than later, your peace of mind will again be troubled by the author, with other tales about you, and us, *dreamers* all, desirous of running away from the hell we call home.

Femi Ojo-Ade

Homeward Bound

"Hello, operator, could you help me with this number, please? The direct line doesn't seem to be through. It's 493-9947, area code 416."

"Thank you, I'll dial it for you... There, you are through now, go ahead."

"Thanks a lot, operator. Hello, may I speak to Ade, please?"

"This is he. Ah, brother, *kini nkan*?"

"All right, I guess, how about you?"

"Everything is fine up here, although I am having a tough time preparing for my exams, as usual. You sound rather low, bros, what is the matter?"

"Hmm, haven't you heard the latest from home? There are new complications in the political situation back there, and I received a signal today asking me to return at once. In fact, I hear that all officers overseas are being recalled."

"My goodness! What a lousy situation! If I were you, brother, I would not move an inch. No way! And, that is my advice to you, if you care to know."

"I'm not calling to seek your advice, because I have been given my orders, and I'm not about to disobey them. I'm calling only to inform you of my imminent departure. But, I really wonder what is happening back home..."

"That is exactly what I mean. You see, you're not even sure yourself. I sense some doubt deep in your mind."

"Hell, no!!! Don't ever make such a mistake. I'm going back, no doubt about that. I am only worried about the general condition in the society. Everything from over there appears very sketchy. For example, a general mobilization may be going on and, if so, civilians may be involved in the process."

"Brother *mi*, don't you think about that at all! Whether or not civilians are involved, just count me out of it. And, please, take my advice,

1

do not go!!! There are various ways of avoiding that trip. You could obtain a doctor's report; you could pretend not to have received the so-called signal. You should forget about that country for some time. Come up here, or go underground, and that is a very easy thing to do around here. Jesus Christ! This is why I was so mad when you decided to join the army. You..."

"Okay, okay, spare me the sermon, dear little brother. Come on now, don't be funny. You cannot hide forever. I have a conscience and am dedicated to my profession and nation. I've got to go, and that is final. I wish you and the rest the best of luck."

After the phone discussion, he was not feeling very well, so he lay down on his sofa and went to sleep. His phone rang. It was his younger friend returning his earlier call, trying again, desperately, to dissuade him from returning home. But he was bent on obeying military orders, and working towards everlasting peace and prosperity for his dear nation. The second discussion did not last nearly as long as the first. He gave his friend no chance to talk; it would have been an unnecessary waste of precious time. Soon after, he fell back into a sleep filled with dreams.

He relived his glorious days at Sandhurst where he won a medal as the best cadet in the whole of the British Commonwealth of Nations. Days of hard drills. Days of long exercises and military maneuvers. Endless mock battles. Sleepless nights with backache and other pains. Real war experience in the Congo. Other training stints in Germany and Ethiopia. Pride. Satisfaction. Pain. Suffering. Progress. Success.

He was back home within one week, fully prepared for action on the front. The authorities were careful to avoid using words such as, war, destruction, and death. Those words were considered too negative, and liable to destroy the nation's morale. Instead, a positive vocabulary was developed, such as, national construction, purge, police action, cleaning up the motherland, forging unity and harmony in diversity. Nothing said about *civil war*.

He had always found it difficult to face the stark realities of life in his native Benue. His abbreviated, barely-more-than-a-year absence had further removed him from those realities. Corruption, confusion, and conspiracy, he thought, were qualities of fools, and he could not believe that the nation's leaders, proud beneficiaries of proper British training, could exhibit such low characteristics.

His arrival at the airport went without any incident. The prominent message, posted on Independence Day a decade before, was still there, high on the terminal building, alone, and symbolic:

WELCOME TO THE REPUBLIC OF BENUE
WHERE FAITH, UNITY, CHARITY, AND KINSHIP
REIGN SUPREME

The only change noticeable about the sign, and the building, was the brown hue replacing the lily-white original color used on that first, long forgotten day. It was evident that a decade of existence without renovation was taking its toll on the signboard, the building, and everything else in the great nation.

He met other returning military officers at the airport. Glum faces oozing fear, they were far from representing the mythical Benue citizen who, in many a visitor's opinion, must be sniffing laughing gas every blessed day. He was also struck by the sea of uniforms swarming all over the building.

"Security," as one fellow-officer remarked, "is of high priority now."

He and the others were driven in a Mercedes straight to the Lugard Garrison where general deployment of officers and strategic plans, were taking place.

He did not get to see his mother and father for two weeks after his arrival. The meeting, when it finally occurred, was rather brief. No time for petty family talk when national responsibilities were waiting.

His father and mother were brought to the barracks in an army jeep that had waited for them at the motor-park. They were both covered with dust. Their faces, etched in stoic resignation, could hardly hide the long suffering and sadness endemic in the lives of those whose children had not had enough time to fully care for them. Sad faces, yet devoid of any selfish complaints. Their concern, as always, was mainly for their only son's safety.

Father smiled proudly at the sight of his uniformed and decorated son. He patted him lightly on his burly shoulders. Mother did not smile, she just kept asking her son over and over again:

"When are you going to come back home for good?"

It was exactly the same question she had put to him years earlier, when he returned from his first overseas training. Seeing him brought back memories of that other reunion but, more poignantly, those of his first days in the army.

"Why go into that life of violence and death? There are many better vocations, you know. Medicine; your uncle is a medical doctor. Engineering; your cousin is a successful engineer. Law; your aunty is one of the first female lawyers in the country. Journalism; your father himself used to be a highly reputed newspaper man."

"But, mama, those people led, and are leading, their own lives. They are doing what they want to do. Me, I want to be in the army. I made up my mind since the time I was a cadet in the secondary school. Our country is now free, and we need a strong army. Defense is one of the most important aspects of every great nation's life, and I wish to be part of that."

"My son, you talk of nation, of independence, as if those things mean anything here. Define them for me, if you can! We, your parents, know that the white man will continue to control us for many years to come and, in the army, it will be the same. The so-called leaders have always been subservient to the whites, and that will not change even in your own time. White man's clothes, white man's ideas, white man's lies."

"Don't worry, mama, I shall travel to many beautiful places, and send you pretty gifts. And, let me assure you, I shall not die in any war. All right? I shall become a useful citizen of this country, and you and papa will be proud of me."

The wise woman was not deceived by the sweet, filial talk. She did not insist that he define terms that she herself found meaningless.

His father had been proud of him for many years. During all his journeys, his pictures regularly appeared in *The Daily Herald Tribune*, the newspaper for which the old man worked. "Papa General," that is, the general's father, as he used to be known by colleagues, readers and friends, personally wrote articles extolling his son's accomplishments. Only "Mama General" could not see why the road to death should be paved with praise and sham glory.

The short visit to the barracks was the very last meeting between son and parents. Before their departure, father and mother gave their son a box of strange articles meant to protect him against any danger on the war front. The box was to be kept under his bed at all times. The father showed him a set of beads that must be worn on his neck twenty-four hours a day. The proud soldier took the whole package, reluctantly.

4

The following day, he led a battalion to the Highland Garrison, the last stop for soldiers going to give and take real bullet. The garrison commander was an old superior of his, but a very friendly one. Major-General "Beauty-Pass-Money" was a ladies' man, and he and the new arrival used to have great times together in the Congo. Beauty had a lady friend at every port of call, and a bed in every corner of the country. He had no wife, legally. It was common knowledge, however, that he had fathered several children. To maintain his military and social dignity, Beauty had a regular female house guest. At least, so he claimed. The guest's period of welcome varied from one day without a night -a record for speed- to nine months, another record, for endurance. The latest guest held the record for the latter.

She was exceptionally pretty. Her face was symmetrically coated with make-up which she did not really need. Her perfume, generously applied, could be smelt from a thousand miles away. Her hair was jet black and very long. Her complexion was smooth and clear, thanks to the miracles of *ambi*, the popular skin-tone cream. A set of snow-white denture dazzled her interlocutor, as did her very upright, enhanced bust line. Her "general" showed her off at every occasion. He also assigned two hefty body-guards to keep her intact and untouched by other hands.

She was introduced to the newly arrived younger officer at the mess, two days after his arrival at the garrison. She could not take her eyes off him. Later, back at the military mansion occupied by Beauty, she could not take her mind off the younger officer.

She could not help asking Beauty for what she called some vital information, on an officer she had never seen in her life. Beauty did not appreciate her badly concealed interest, and chided her militarily, with a whip. She avoided further punishment by turning her shrill cry into a loud snore.

Beauty, a man of honor ready to combat any affront on his integrity -at least, so he claimed- never forgot the incident.

He gave instructions for the new unit to move to the war-front, with immediate effect. The junior officer and the object of the woman's affection, or affected emotions, found it strange that his unit was being moved ahead of several that had preceded them to the garrison; but, orders were orders. Nonetheless, he complained to Beauty about his men's lack of experience and preparations. As a compensatory measure, Beauty ordered more men from the garrison to be added to the departing unit. *To keep the nation clean is a task that must be done, with alacrity.*

"I am giving you our best sharp-shooters, the most courageous of the lot, the most trustworthy soldiers this garrison can boast of." Major-General Beauty-Pass-Money smiled from ear to ear.

The younger officer expressed his sincere gratitude to the man of beauty, and assured his men that all was, and would be, well.

We are fighting, fighting, fighting
Fighting for the nation,
We are going, going, going
Going for the nation.
Goodbye Papa, goodbye Mama,
Keep the notion, notion, notion
Notion of Faith, Unity, Charity, and Kinship.
F is for Faith, U is for Unity,
C is for Charity, K is for Kinship,
F.U.C.K!!!
To keep the nation clean
Is a task that must be done.

They all sang loud and clear. They looked proud together, and determined to go clean up the great nation. He stood at attention beside Beauty as they both reviewed the marching battalion. He looked directly into the ugly man's eyes. He did not like what he saw, as the man, for the first and last time, avoided eye-to-eye contact with his inferior officer.

For the first time in his career, he wondered whether he would return from the war front. Beauty smiled and shook hands with him, more warmly than ever before.

"See you later, and be careful, you hear?"

Among the sparse crowd of onlookers was Beauty's guest, the record-breaker that had been at the receiving end of the Major-General's whip, and the lover that the younger officer never knew, and would never know. She was looking straight at the object of her affection, or of affected emotions, and appearing to say to him something secret, but incomprehensible. Beauty noticed the little drama. He shook his head, and smiled again. Everything was under control, someone's control, but surely not the woman's, nor the departing officer's.

6

When are you going to come back home for good? The question echoed in his mind, one more time. Before jumping into the seat next to the truck driver, he hit his left toe hard against a stone, stumbled, and had to struggle to regain his balance.

"Sorry, sah, sorry, sah," stammered the driver.

"Nothing at all, thank you. Let's go."

The national clean-up was not an easy task, not as easy as the optimistic and patriotic leaders had thought, and announced to the public. It was war. It was hell. Brothers were killing brothers like Christmas chickens, or Ramadan rams. Poor, innocent people were maimed and murdered. Insanity reigned supreme, and the criminals at the helm of power, thousands of miles away from combat, attained earthly glory as national heroes.

He was among the handful who maintained their sanity; who refused to benefit from other people's woes; who stuck doggedly to the military code of conduct. He fought valiantly. His father was proud to report news about his exploits as they reached the city from the war front. His troops were rapidly advancing into the hinterland, cleaning up the land, and keeping the nation one, according to the dictates of the masters leisurely sipping their wine and women back in the peaceful city. Both the leaders and the press proclaimed the successful defense of the nation's unity. Only a few lives were lost, so said officialdom, and new heroes were mushrooming by the day with stories of extraordinary courage. Every act of courage was worth another one, as lies mingled with truth or, indeed, gained the upper hand.

After one very bitterly fought battle, the newly promoted Colonel, the real hero, retreated to his quarters. *When are you going to come back home for good?* He undressed quietly, removed his beads from his neck, and placed them in the box containing his other protective paraphernalia. He began to whistle an old army tune, took his towel, and walked briskly to the bathroom. Images of his mother and father were suddenly passing before his eyes. He smiled confidently, certain that he would soon see them again.

They found his bullet-riddled naked body the following morning, lying face down on the bathroom floor. The sharp-shooters chosen by Beauty to augment his battalion's strength, had used him for target practice.

Papa and Mama General were given the news by an officer who

tried very hard to show sympathy. Their son's body was never returned home. The officer claimed that it had been buried in the war front. His mother vowed to have it dug up and buried in the family plot. She would try, unsuccessfully, until her dying day.

Visitors to the house could not talk to her of anything, or anyone else but her son.

"He is finally going to come home," she kept muttering under her breath.

An American Dream

"Dis America sef, na wa o, my broda."

"Yeah, yeah, and you can say that again, man."

"All dis yuah Americana lingo, wetin dey wrong wit you? ma man, mon, men, nonsense! Simple, absolute nonsense!"

"Make una go slow on im now, bobo. Ah, wit all dis wahala for dis nonsense country, why una dey go quarrel like dat?"

"Don't mind the stupid man. He's forever bitching about America, yet he's been here for ages. And..."

"Shut up yuah big mout, *so gbo*! See wuh dey talk sef. You *nko*, ow many year you don spend, foty, fity? *Abi* na you bring me ere?"

"Oh, wow! why can't you ever understand me? I'm here to make a living, man, that's all. And you, too, you have gotta get that into your thick skull. You seem to forget I was home recently. Oh, yeah, that was a real shitty country for you, dirt, disease, all over the goddamn place."

"See am, see wuh dey talk skol! You get anytin foh yuah ead at all? Ow many day you spend foh Niger to now come and bool-sheet the place? Eh, eh! No be Mexico you go sef? *Abi* you don begin lie now?"

"Okay, okay, my brodas, make una no dey fight now. *Sebi* una see ow tins dey go foh we, *abi* una no dey see? Let me cut una anoda drink, make we use am drown our sorrow. Ere, take am, Uncle Sam... And you, too, Eddie... Make I poh some foh de ancestohs... Make dem wash ofah us o, make dem lead us back ome in peace and prosparity."

"I say a-a-a-men to that! My, oh my, this stuff is dope, man, I tell ya. I just love the lager from way back home. You know, all the time I was back there..."

"E don come again o, dope dope! *Abi* you dey smoke sottin? Ehem, Baba, dis boy na danger o. Wit all de tory we eah of Niger people, de lords and dere curios..."

"What the hell is he saying? I'm talking of the quality of this bad, bad beer from back home. I tell you, Eddie, don't start dissing me, don't you ever, or else I'm gonna..."

"*Se* you people no won ear me *ni*? We get to tok important tings and na fight una dey fight."

"All right, all right, but, man, that guy's behavior is real cold, I mean, cold, man, cold!"

"If you get col for summah time, you betta go ospital."

"Eh, eh, oga Eddie, dat's enuff now!"

Thus started another summer day in the life of the three African men lost like many others in the civilized society of social security numbers. Their meeting-point, aptly named *the African Miracle*, was a bar in the black sector of a city best called a prison where black blended with the hellish horizon populated by prostitutes and pimps. And those words don't refer to professionals, but to victims of a system that makes people prey upon one another like vultures and vampires. You are free to feed on the feces of the filthy rich. You are most welcome to capitalize on your friends' failings, to triumph through their tragedies, to go up and come down, or run round and round in the glorified ghetto of capitalism. For, hopes of the Great Dream are constantly alive, thrown at you in the newspapers and on television. And you cannot recall how long you've been hoping for heaven in hell.

Baba, Eddie and Sam arrived years ago. None of them seemed to (want to?) know exactly when. By the time they had had enough beer to sink a ship crossing the Atlantic on its way back to their beloved home, the question of how long would inadvertently come up and, naturally, the year would change according to each one's flight of fancy, or their collective composure, or amnesia. On that particular day, Baba appeared much troubled. His blood-shot eyes, permanently dilated after a decade of catching taxi-customers in dark corners in his unlicensed rickety car, his eyes were dancing desperately, the speed of movement from Eddie's puffy, pimpled face to Sam's seemingly satisfied demeanor, increasing in unison with the rhythm of his speech, and the flow of lager beer down the throat.

"My wife is a daty dog!" Baba spat out in disgust. Sudden silence, except for the clatter of empty bottles being cleared by Mr. Miracle himself. Slowly, very slowly, water was welling in Baba's eyes. The tears started streaming down, two parallel lines of equal quality of tragedy and despair. Like twins entangled from the womb in a double dose of kindness, or cruelty. Like wives of the polygamist caught in a web of their master's monstrosities, or blessed with a commonality of care and concern. Like blacks of the world walking in their various ways through the dastardly desert of living death.

"My wife dey sleep wit my broda, de broda wey ah bring wit my money to dis contree. Wetin a go do now, tell me, wetin!"

Eddie smiled weirdly, shook his head, and told the man to cut him another drink.

Sam told him to shut up, that he was trying to think. If he hadn't said so, one would have been convinced that he was falling asleep. But, yes, he was thinking quite all right, thinking of that journey he had just made to Mexico, or wherever, with his darling wife.

Everyone in the African community knew Sam was an expert in women matters, given his problematic experience, and his most brave and manly way of resolving it. But if only they all knew the truth...

Sam was once a womanizer, running after anything in a dress or high heels and, most importantly, American. He used to tell his compatriots that, for him, the most practical payment any white country could cough up for Africa's history of enslavement and colonialism, was to witness their women's beautiful bodies wriggling in a bed blackened by the body of one of those that they had been dehumanizing for centuries. And Sam never stopped telling and re-telling with modifications dictated by his mood-swing, the tale of his arrival at the Great Society's welcoming airport: He came with only the shirt on his back, and declared himself a refugee from "a jungle dictatorship" thousands of miles away. The immigration officer, a blonde heart-stopper with a toothy, plastic smile, showed immediate sympathy, willing and able as she was to save "the poor savage from Africa." Sam ended up spending several nights at her apartment! Another version of the story, told with less glee on dreary days of unspecified misfortune and slow movement of beer to mouth, had him arriving with a lot of money, and sweeping one of the hostesses on his flight off her feet.

The most patent truth was that Sam was now in money, a lot of money, without working at any known job. The increase in means -of course, it was the realization of everyone's dream- was complemented by the Americanization of his manners. Finally, Sam spoke only in slang. He had successfully extricated himself from the pidgin common among his people back there in the home which he often denied when questioned by strangers.

Then, suddenly, Sam announced one day that he was going home to bring back a wife worthy of him. His two best friends, Baba and Eddie, didn't believe until he phoned them to come and meet his new "madam." Madam was hardly an adult. Big, bulging eyes truly befitting a well endowed body that would keep the man busy all night long. Madam was full of life and respect. Not surprisingly, all of Sam's African compatriots were easily won over by that beauty, unspoiled by capitalism, and trained to be hospitable to all comers. Sam's house was always full of well-wishers celebrating Madam's arrival long after the couple had settled into the life of lies expected of responsible people.

Soon enough, mouths began to wag about Madam's generosity.

When Sam caught her warmly welcoming in bed one of his much younger compatriots, he openly blamed himself for not being up to the task of satisfying his beloved Madam. Everyone wondered what type of man would desist from meting out well deserved death to an impatient intruder unable to arrange his need for warmth at a clandestine, stop-over motel, rather than stealing into the poor husband's bed. Only a cool cat, a truly wise man like Sam could condone such an insult.

After that incident, Sam became more generous than ever before to Madam. He even missed quite a few appointments at *the African Miracle*. Baba, unable to make the trip back home, soon followed Sam's lead and took a mail-order bride. The woman arrived with his younger brother.

"Sam, Uncle Sammie, na sleep una dey sleep now?"

"Come on, man, I tell ya I'm thinking, thinking, thin-kiiinnng! Can't you understand simple, straightforward English? You just messed up my thoughts!"

Baba was apologetic and feeling inferior, as he usually did in Sam's presence. Eddie was too drunk to put in his little bit of criticism. Sam slipped back into his world of secrets.

The African hero feted and fawned upon his Madam like a new Cadillac, or one of those Mercedes clogging the streets of his country where majority of the people could not afford one meal per day while their saviors and messiahs were religiously saving millions of dollars into their personal accounts abroad, as a means of preparing the people for better life in paradise. Madam did, indeed, feel like a Mercedes, all shining and sparkling clean. Only the strange man refused to ride her.

The first night he crept into their bed that he had abandoned after her harmless show of hospitality towards the young compatriot, Madam was waiting, really waiting to prove to her man that he was the one and only, the lord and master of his kingdom. She was wearing the new night-gown bought by him as a token of his forgiveness. He knew she wasn't used to wearing those things in bed. He knew she did it just for him.

He lay by her side and announced plans for a trip to Mexico. A kind of honeymoon, according to him. But why Mexico? she wondered to herself. They said they spoke Spanish there. Why not U.K., United Kingdom, the dream-land of everyone back home long before America became the craze? She dared not voice her opinion lest Sam get angry and leave the bed.

After his announcement, he turned his back on poor Madam and started to snore rather loudly.

Sam informed his friends of the honeymoon journey. In Mexico, he would love to see Acapulco and, possibly, he'd take his Madam down to Brazil for the carnival. The journey became headline news at *the African Miracle*. Sam did the unimaginable: He took Madam to the bar, to parade her before his people, to show her as symbol of a well maintained wife, like those Mercedes cars coveted by armed robbers back home who would kill just to ride and abandon one after using it to commit crimes unheard of in a country priding itself on its exemplary human principles.

The plane was about to take off, destination Lagos, when Madam learnt that Mexico was a dreamland to the south of America, and Brazil, another impossible dream farther south. It was, however, too late to get off. Sam convinced her that he meant to make it a surprise, that they were actually going home to perform the traditional wedding rites, the lack of which had led to that episode of harmless hospitality with the young compatriot.

Madam became abandoned property at the Lagos airport. Sam warned her not to try to follow him. If she did, he would disgrace her forever. He didn't even have the courtesy to return her to her parents who had given her to him in good faith.

"I tink I weel keel dat boy! I weel stragle eem! I don care, broda or no broda. Sam, tell me now, wetin make I do, wetin?"

Eddie was snoring noisily and rhythmically, and a faint smile was slowly appearing on his chubby cheeks, the only round part of his body besides the belly pregnant with beer. It was the snoring, not Baba's plea, that forced Sam to return to the reality of *the Miracle*.

"Well, well, we'll think of something. I'm not sure your kid brother is to blame, although... Eh, you lazy-bones, wake up, man, wake up!"

Eddie had just begun to enjoy his own dream of days in the doldrums of his African ivory-tower turned into hopes of happiness in the much revered land of honey where, too late for him, the dream died like flowers withered by winter and like a sane man suddenly become mad. But Eddie's story would have to wait.

Sam shook him out of his sleep. They cussed out each other, as usual. And, as usual, Uncle Sam had the last word. He promised to go visit Baba at home that evening, with what he called a master-plan to solve his problem. Baba laughed for the very first time that day.

"Uncle Sameee! I know am, I know you go get to solf de tin foh me."

The three dreamers, call them the dealer, the don and the driver, staggered out into the sweltering summer heat.

No Condition is Permanent

It was a usual scene at the capital. The main streets were filled with crawling cars whose horns competed for supremacy with the sweet sounds emitted by the surging crowd, emerging from nowhere and going nowhere in particular. Vendors of all ilks were hawking drugs, clothing, books, and foodstuffs made more palatable by flies preying upon them on the sidewalks. Several jobless laggards were whistling at the eye-catching skirts wriggling by. A girl was cursing a confused boy's progenitors, and the boy's friend stood by and laughed excitedly. On another street-corner, a professional beggar, blind by day and blessed with perfect eyesight by night, held out his big bowl into which almost everyone threw a coin. The beggar knew exactly how much he was given by each generous compatriot and blessed them accordingly. Some young bank employees, choking under the knot of their protruding, colorful ties, were discussing politics in a very loud fashion. "I'm so happy we have had another coup. Those bastards didn't know what they were doing."

"I don't know, I just don't know. Maybe all these coups are not good for the nation. Maybe we need more stability. Three coups within a year, that's too much!"

"But I think it is fantastic! That's what they call progress. Just look at the wealth of our great nation. The faster the change of government, the faster the wealth will circulate and rotate."

"Yeah, chop make I chop. I for one expect the present government to be out within six months at the most."

"Nonsense, arrant nonsense! How do you mean? This regime is exceptional. I wish they would be in there for a long, long time."

"Ah, ah, I'm not surprised, your brother is now a minister. The longer the better!"

"Don't mistake him for a despotic jackass. I myself feel that this is a good government. They are moving in the right direction, and we

15

should all give them a chance. But, at least, let them increase wages, build more roads, improve education, give us more amenities, industrialize the whole country, improve the poor man's lot, stamp out corruption, nepotism, dictatorship, and communism, evolve a real African ideology, and remove our great nation from under the rotten umbrella of colonialism."

"Well, well, but you say this is a good government."

"Don't get him wrong, he means this government has potential."

"But what have they done to date?"

"They are building a national stadium, a national museum, a national highway, a national radio network, a national everything!"

"And, remember this is a totally civilian government."

"Yes, yes, a military government in mufti."

A few passers-by cast a glance at the "intellectuals" endowed with fast tongues and fast heads and very much concerned with their nation's destiny. But the shouting match was hardly noticed by most of the crowd engaged in providing, each in his own personal way, for their various national needs, repeating acts that constitute their life six days a week. Sunday was a holy day and everybody, including the loquacious bankers, took time off.

The scene at the capital was naturally a microcosm of the national scene of happiness and dedication to one's task, and each task was valuable, and necessary.

If the young bankers and certain other "intellectuals" were always concerned with Sahara's future, they took consolation in their conviction that the mighty desert was much better than any other country in Africa. That was the consensus of opinion among all citizens, male and female, adult and young, and children, too.

The new government was building upon that consolatory fact; a wise move, indeed. The new President constantly stressed the need for a positive outlook, and national effort. "We must go to the people," Mr. President often said to his followers. And to the people he had been going since his take-over two months before. He used to get drunk on imported beer with the "intellectual" *habitués* of the capital's Westernized hotels. And they were there in large numbers: the Hilton, the Sheraton, the Watergate, the Méridien, and others. The President used to eat pounded yam with his hands, and to drink palm-wine out of a calabash with "uncouth" locals crowded into thatched-roofed bars.

He would pay homage to the street-women in their fun-providing havens. He would visit God in His house, and would appease the traditional gods with sacrifice and regular calls at the babalawo's shrine. He increased the number of his familiar entourage, especially female bodies. He ordered a long, long open-top limousine and rode tirelessly among the people, his own people. Of course, in order for many people to peacefully enjoy their leader's presence, the streets had to be regularly cleared an hour beforehand by fierce-looking dispatch-riders. He had street names changed in honor of national heroes, the current ones, naturally, that is, his own humble self and a few others, precisely, his friends and associates.

His people loved him, adored him, and deified him. Everything was done in the name of Sahara. Everything done was good for Sahara. Every good thing for Sahara started and ended with him.

Mr. President's people did not include certain recalcitrant, rebellious terrorists. Like a chronic disease, those divisive elements, naturally abhorred by the people, his people, would rear their gory heads, and aim at the destruction of the beloved nation. Plotters of coups. Harbingers of conflict. Purveyors of polarization. Every president in Sahara had to deal with them, and the current messiah was bent upon successfully carrying out his glorious program over the dead bodies of any unpatriotic elements standing in his way. With his People's Movement, he had driven the disruptive elements underground in a matter of days. With his regular radio and television broadcasts, he was making the people aware of his realistic, patriotic program, for the realization of peace, prosperity, and progress.

"No more coups in this great nation of ours! My people, my coming to power is a providential event, I can assure you of that. From now on, not a single case of bloodshed shall be condoned in this great nation. Let us move forward in our quest for prosperity and unity. My happy people, God is with us in our task. If you are a Christian, make churchgoing a regular part of your life. If you are a Moslem, make the mosque your home, and if you are a believer in our forefathers' religion, use their powers for the good of this great nation of ours. As I have already stated, my ascent to power is God's doing, not mine. So, my own people, my good people, let us praise Him. With His help, our task is already made easy, no doubt about it. Let all enemies of this great nation flee the devil and return to God. This is the end of bloodshed and the beginning of a new day."

The same theme had been repeated for two months, at gatherings, on the radio, on television, everywhere. And the people's enemies were disappearing into the devil's hell at a fast rate. And the price of milk went soaring even as Mr. President was launching a new program to feed the nation's children with milk. And the press reported a loss in Sunday-service contributions all over the great nation. And many bodies, worthy sacrificial lambs, were found at many crossroads. And the nation's future was exceedingly bright. And the people, Mr. President's own people, were very happy, with their increasingly empty stomachs and increasing danger of death.

President Oloje sat in his study drafting a new constitution, indeed, a people's constitution. It was dark outside on a cool Sunday evening. There was movement somewhere in the marble-structure that he had built and baptized *the people s palace*. It had to be one of the servants getting ready to go home. The President had to concentrate on the task at hand, a very important, national task. Hence, he detested such unwarranted disturbance. His thoughts skipped through the attitude and character of his faithful servants, above all, that of his bodyguard, Alimi. A neighbor's son from his village, Alimi had been taken away from his clerical position and had himself chosen the other members of the palace-guard. All of them were hard-working, totally honest, and trustworthy.

The President heard the noise again. Unable to countenance the disturbance any longer, he called out Alimi's name.

No answer.

He returned to his heavy, patriotic task.

Another strange noise was echoed very close to the walls of the study. Mr. President was not in the least worried. Everything would soon die down, he thought. He was trying to work out the items of a section of the constitution that would incorporate life presidency into the Saharan system. Other wise nations on the continent were doing it. A great president needed a life-time to fully implement his great program. The fruition of a program worthy of the name depended upon continuity. His predecessors were not intelligent enough to think of that; not surprising, since none of them was qualified to man the post. The nation had been awaiting the arrival of a real messiah, to embark upon a long-term scheme of development and modernization. Sahara was fortunate to have him, the right man for the right job, coming at the right moment.

His pen was moving smoothly on the paper and he was by then totally deaf to the bothersome noise outside the room.

A gentle breeze blew through the open window and brought back to his mind thoughts of student days spent on the shores of the big coastal cities of foreign lands. But the thoughts died out quickly. The national task must not be disturbed.

A fly, big and black, buzzed at his ears. He gently drove it off with his left hand.

He had to finish the task at hand, a very important task, a national task, a task on which the people's destiny depended.

Suddenly, the door flew open, and in rushed a distraught-looking Alimi.

"Dey are comin for you, sah!"

"What is all this nonsense about, Alimi? What's the reason for all this stupid uproar? Can't you knock anymore before you enter? And, by the way..."

"Dey are comin, sah, dey are comin for you!"

"Who's coming for you? Are you mad, or something? Why are you shaking all over? Are you sick, or what? Tell me, what's the meaning of all this?!"

"Sah, dey are ere, sah, I tink you shud give up *jeje*. Dere's notin you can do oderwise now, sah. Dey are comin, comin for you, sah..."

"Alimi, listen to me! I'm going to get mad at you in a second. Can't you see I am trying to do some very urgent work for our nation? And why should you come in here and disturb me? Why couldn't you phone the secretary if there are any VIPs coming up to the residence?"

"De phone is out of odah, sah. And dat is not going to elp anyone, sah. Dere is notin any of us can do now."

"OK, shut up!!! Get out of this place!!! But, what's coming over you? Tell me, have you forgotten the son of whom you are? Or, can't you recognize me anymore? It is me, your own brother, your master, your savior, telling you to obey instructions!!!"

Something seemed to have swept away the servant's fear. For the first time during their relationship, the servant put on an air of self-confidence and control.

"Now, shot up, mister man!!! I am tell you, I dey give you odah to do as I say one time. Bettah be ready to go wit me now now. No more ank-ing-panking. If you no take time, I go take de law into my and right now!"

"But, but, Alimi, you must be sick, you are sick, you ARE ill... Let me, let me..."

"I say, shot up!!!"

"Please, please, Alimi, please, I will give you whatever you want, anything at all, just name it. Clothes, cash, a car, whatever it will take, I'm prepared to give it to you. Just let me finish this great task before me."

As was the case with the man before him, Mr. President's courage melted once he realized that he was running the risk of losing the opportunity to save his life. He went down on his knees, joined his shaky hands together, and his cowardly lips began to shower songs of praise upon his erstwhile servant. The latter was relentless. He grew less understanding and more abusive with each newly uttered word.

"I dey tell you fool dat it is time to go!!! De day of reckon done come, and it is your time to go. Like de odahs before you, it is time to sacriface for de good of dis nation. You wan buy me to your side, so you bring me to de palace. A safant! Your safant! And you call me your broda. Is dat de job of a broda? Jus go to ell, *jo*!!!"

Mr. President crawled nervously towards the circular waterbed placed in a corner of the large study. He took a key from under the pillow. Alimi snatched it from his hand, made a threatening move from which the master recoiled, and spat, first on the ground and then flush on the face of the father of the nation.

"You wan open the gate of ell?"

"Lord, no, Alimi, oh no! I just want to make you an offer, a well-deserved one, I can assure you."

Alimi gave him the key and he leapt like a monkey towards a safe in the corner. His trembling hands held open the door. Stacks of hard currency were staring them both in the face.

"We will divide all this into two equal parts if you just let me go, please."

"Shot up, I tell you!!!"

The servant's voice broke, momentarily. He swallowed his anger for a long minute. He felt the new notes piled in front of him. He smelt them with relish. His hands began to shake. The notes were real, clean, countless, and shining, crisp, something he had never dreamt of seeing in his dastardly life. The national passport to heaven on earth.

"I go take every tin!!!"

"But, but you can't do that, Alimi, my dear Alimi, hein, you can't do that to me. Remember, our watchword has always been unity. We have to share, like brothers that we are."

Alimi, angered once again, pushed Mr. President onto his knees and ordered him to lick his torn shoes. The master obeyed with alacrity. That done, the servant spat once more on the frightened face.

"Okay, I go take de money and keep it save. We go chare it equally, as you don say. Dat is a promise."

The servant slammed the door of the safe, turned the lock, and pocketed the key. He pulled the curtain, thus concealing the trove from any intrusive eyes, as if he was the master.

"But, Alimi, I don't have to go anywhere. I don't..."

Other footsteps, loud, authoritative, and threatening, were approaching the room. Alimi jumped on Mr. President and started to roughen him up while shouting obscenities at his spittle-laden face. Four nation-conscious, gun-toting gentlemen entered and snatched Mr. President away from Alimi's claws. They did not want him hurt. They still respected him. One of them even greeted him with a polite "sah." They chided the servant for molesting a whole Head of State, a whole father of the nation, and threatened to discipline the cantankerous young man. They promised to cater to the President's needs and interests. He was in danger of losing his life to the whims of some idiot with quick hands and with mud in his brain. He was to be taken away for his own safety. He was still their President, and nothing was ever going to change that.

They marched out of the room with Mr. President protectively sandwiched in the middle. Alimi remained behind.

The Saharan capital awoke on Monday morning to the usual hustle and bustle of a new week and the ever increasing challenges for those millions struggling to survive. Thousands of vehicles, many of them rare models imported from faraway lands, zigzagged their way down the undulating, pot-holed main arteries. Horns were fighting to be heard among the human roars and yelps. Jobless, patriotic streetwalkers and sleep-walkers, hawkers of odds and ends, spectators of non-spectacles, early risers all, wended their way to the city's center.

The professional beggars, their big bowls still empty, a rarity, were beginning their call for generosity and kindness as they mixed prayers with gibberish. Some penny-throwing pupils, their books loaded on the smallest one's head, were shouting their way merrily to school. Young bankers in woolen suits and ties fit for the neck of an armed robber, were going to the office in twos and threes, whispering something about the quality of the new regime.

Everyone was going about their own business. Everyone was continuing to live as they could, as they should, as if nothing had happened. Everyone was happy, as usual, in their own way, patriotically, naturally.

By night, some lives would have changed, inevitably. Bodies disappearing. Some new faces in new places. Some old faces in the same place. Better bargaining power for new VIPs. Worse weather for some socially drought-ridden miscasts and miscreants. The usual promise of better days ahead for a people caught asleep in the belly of the beast.

A sudden, total stop in the traffic caught every eager eye. Model spectators all, Saharans hurried to the scene. It was an accident between a late-model car and a battered lorry with a caption on its side. The radio in the car was broadcasting the national news, and the report, hardly audible to anyone in the thickening crowd, was that the President would soon talk to the nation, on radio and television. According to the female voice hardly hiding a certain joy, the ousted pretender had disappeared. Since the lorry was lying on its side, the writing could have been difficult to read, yet nobody had a problem reading it; even the illiterates could guess the message. A young man, an almost burnt-out cigarette dangling from his mouth, and his three-piece suit serving as facilitator and terminator of the sweat drenching his whole body, shouted out the caption to no one in particular, and a mischievous laughter split his broad face from ear to ear.

NO CONDITION IS PERMANENT.

Wedding Bells

Their meeting and ultimate decision to marry each other were due as much to the elements as to their personal sentiments.

That winter was particularly severe. Like many winters since his arrival at Three Rivers three years before, it started rather early. Snow fell heavily and many houses were almost turned into domiciliary icebergs. However, unlike other winters, that one was marked by numerous stormy days and nights. His neighbors told him it was the first time in memory that lives were lost in a snowstorm, and that was repeated on several occasions that winter.

The Riverians usually expressed their love for the rather cold winter to every newcomer, and he never doubted their sincerity. Indeed, he himself needed only one winter away from his native tropics to develop a deep affection for the cold paradise. That winter, however, love turned into hate and several well-greened citizens, for once in their lives, packed their little flight-bags and sneaked off to the Caribbean. Nature, they claimed, had begun to play tricks on mere mortals. Spring came symbolically -the date, like Christmas, never changes- but snow continued to fall, with the attendant cold biting hard at helpless, innocent bodies. He who runs away lives to fight another day. The Riverian runners had at their disposal the plane, man's fastest mode of transportation, and they ran in their hundreds, leaving behind the cold, and the poor African.

For the first time he, too, missed home. He remembered those hot days when he used to walk about in his shirt-tails, when he used to sit down on the beach and read a Shakespearean play. He recalled the cold water from his grandmother's big pot; the water was as cold as any taken from the best refrigerator. He remembered the long nights under the full moon, with nature's light setting everything aglow for miles around.

Nonetheless, he could not return home because of the so inclement winter. Not until he had achieved his goal: a university degree. The one positive aspect of the especially harsh weather was that it made him concentrate on his studies, foregoing the sporadic social outings and the infrequent visits to friends in neighboring cities.

The one negative aspect was loneliness. Not even he, a book-worm from his secondary-school days, could help feeling alone, and defeated by nature.

She, too, was exceedingly lonesome. Unlike him, she was not a student. Therefore, the imprisonment brought about by the winter was for her a particularly excruciating experience. On milder days, she could drive out, assured of the firm grip of her snow-tires on the slippery road. But with the storms, driving was out of the question as cars became pebbles easily blown away by the wind. Her stereo set was out of order, and her budget was too tight for her to think of having it fixed. The television, an old black-and-white set, functioned surprisingly well; however, she was tired of watching violent shows after a hard day's work at the hospital. Grumpy old ladies messing up their beds. Proud doctors ordering you around. The nauseating smell of drugs. Faces of death. She needed relaxation. She needed companionship. She needed love.

The storm was most unbearable and frightful that night. She wished she were back in good old England, with her main man, her compatriot from Jamaica, a handsome, light-skinned, and tall Mr. Universe who used to turn her on with his beautiful, well chiseled, muscular body. Just then she needed his protection. Memories came swarming into her mind. Long walks hand in hand in the park, thinking of nothing but love. Plans for a future of fun away from the run-down ghettoes of Kingston town. A dreamland of bliss and fortune. A new fatherland of British dynamism and broadmindedness. Unfortunately, the bubble burst, brusquely: Mr. Universe, wild, unwilling to adapt, unable to accept pale-faced hypocrisy, or to forget the haunting paternalism of their so-called friends, decided to return home to Jamaica. She was dismayed. How could he go back to that jungle? How could he ever think of leaving her, abandoning her? Where was the love? You never go back home to stay! Only to visit.

After the man's departure, she moved across the ocean and settled at Three Rivers.

Three Rivers was not, could never be, London. All the same, it was now home, and she tried to make the best if it. Being a nurse, she met a good number of people, but the small town, like a close family, forestalled freedom and fun. Besides, friends, true friends, were few and far between, especially in a community where color consciousness controlled relationships. Blackness was a rarity in Three Rivers. Now, among blacks, the bond of color was constrained by the cleavage of civilization. You never go back home to stay; only to visit...

The lights went out. She had no candle in her apartment. Her neighbor, the African, was invisible and unfriendly, but she could not stay all by her lonesome in the ghostly darkness.

Why would he prefer to be alone, when all he had to do was walk in through her door? He neither looked happy nor sad. He hardly received visitors, so there was no girl in his life; at least, not in the vicinity. Thus everything pointed to a natural togetherness between two lonely hearts. One of them had to make the move. He did not. She did.

He heard a timid knock on the door.

"Coming... Who is it?"

"It's me, your next-door neighbor. Could you kindly spare a candle? My lights went out just now, and I can't possibly stay in total darkness by..."

"Oh, it's you, miss! Come inside, come inside."

She spent that night in his apartment, on the same bed with him. The passing flame of one night developed into a fire for all times. The spontaneous mating of a stormy night became the permanent bliss of many days and nights. Neighbors saw the union as a natural reconciliation of Africa and her far-flung offspring in the Diaspora. A very civilized logic, no doubt.

Likes attract, opposites repel; another kind of logic.

He saw beyond the fact that she was avowedly much older than he. She was helpful and considerate, a sister through and through.

She in turn saw beyond what she considered as remnants of his retrogressive culture. He was sweet, respectful, and forward-looking. She even managed to develop a sort of love for that homeland where her forefathers had been sold into slavery. She attributed the change of heart to his positive influence, and to her own mellowness.

Their affair moved swiftly towards its culmination at the altar. He left the initiative to her and she did not falter in her every action. Although she expected him to be the aggressor in their affair, she gladly accepted the change of role, convinced as she was that his culture, being different, made the man feel complacent, and superior. Indeed, she thought of asking him a couple of times to explain his Africa to her but, each time, something more important came up. Moreover, she feared being a loser in love and life, for the second time.

He worked assiduously, alone on his books, and with her, in bed. They communicated with their bodies more than with mere words of mouth; a situation which she adored. He expressed not much of a viewpoint either way, showing just the usual, regular assiduity at work. Work came to symbolize willingness, silence, and consent.

A date was set for the wedding: two weeks after his graduation with his Bachelor of Arts degree. It would be a double celebration; academic achievement would be coupled with sentimental fulfillment. A college certificate would be merged with official certification of their everlasting love. In their own very personal way, they were going to realize that dream of harmony in black preached by ideologues of their race all over the globe. Her joy went beyond bounds but -a fact incomprehensible to her- his own joy was somewhat guarded. He assured her nonetheless that his less-than-total happiness was due only to the fact that his people from way back home could not witness the two greatest moments of his life.

One week before the wedding, he asked her to move to her friend's apartment, in order to put the traditional, symbolic distance between man and woman before the final union. She complied with his request. She felt more than ever closer to her roots. Once the ceremony was over, they would live together, happily, forever and evermore.

The landlord was sad to have to find another tenant to replace her, but he was overjoyed that his building had served as the meeting point of two lonely hearts, a good-luck charm for man and woman. In the newspaper advertisement for a new tenant, Mr. Harmony did not forget to state: "The present occupant, a charming, young lady, has just found eternal happiness right in the arms of a gentleman in the same building." Prospective tenants fell over one other, and the lucky one was actually present in church for the auspicious occasion.

She sat there, serene and regal in her flowing white dress. The church was overflowing with friends, as well as readers of newspaper advertisements. They all had the same question on their tongues: Where was the groom?

One of his friends whispered to her not to worry and that, as she well knew, her man was a strong believer in African time. She smiled nervously.

Her waiting, and their curiosity, all was in vain. He never showed up for a wedding which they had consummated months earlier.

While she was waiting in vain at the church, he was on his way to the international airport.

You never go back home again; only to visit... But you may go to visit, you must go to visit, and stay, especially when you have made it in the shade. Teeming throngs meet you at the airport, welcoming you to the land of plenty and poverty. They all are looking up to you. You, the son of the soil. You, the gifted graduate. You, their hero. You, the important intellectual. True sons of the soil never soil their African heritage by returning home with strangers.

As the taxi sped towards the point of departure, he painted in his mind pictures of a political stalwart, a civilized patriot leading his poor people to the promised land of prosperity. Thoughts of her were far from his progressive mind.

The church crowd -did you say, congregation?- was tired of waiting. People began to sneak out in small groups, finally, abandoning her with her bridal train and a body of officials annoyed at the groom's absence. Dilemma gave birth to detestation. Old prejudices, well hidden by civilized hypocrisy, surfaced dramatically.

"Those Africans, they probably never marry this way in their country."

"Imagine! Standing a lady up in the House of God!"

"What a shame! Niggers will forever be niggers."

His friends were not as shocked as the others; for, they knew that marriage was not part of his plan. Indeed, their main goal in attending the ceremony was to verify whether he was going to be there, or keep his promise to bolt.

"That goddamn bastard from the jungle!!!" she sobbed. "I should have known better..."

Snow started to fall outside God's House. Slowly and softly at first. Then in large, hard flakes and, indeed, as hale. One of his friends offered to drive her home. She must not stay in a place that made her mad. She must stop embarrassing herself before those malicious eyes staring at her and mocking her.

She agreed to take his friend's car home.

Destiny

No one was ever broke in the land of plenty, but he was. He once had it made, working two jobs and helping his black brothers and sisters of the Great Society realize their fantasy of a spiritual return to Africa by decking them out in variously shaped dashikis, and selling to them the original reefer from the ancestral home. His two jobs, as a taxi-driver and a security guard, were lucrative, albeit hardly respectable professions, but he quickly learned to view them from the logical, capitalistic perspective. Anything that made money was respectable...

After leaving Africa as a poor tailor imprisoned in a one-room dwelling partitioned by a stinking gutter that he used to spray regularly with air-freshener, his achievement in America was a giant step forward. Almost immediately upon arrival, he had rented a well-furnished apartment, bought a shining, long car, a rack full of fashionable clothes, and made scores of lady-friends. The vaunted golden fleece, mere papers that civilized societies recognized for what they were, soon became a forgotten, useless dream.

He swore that he was never going to return to that poor, backward country of his.

That was ten years ago.

Lately, however, everything had been turning bad. The personnel manager of the security company asked for his work-permit. After days of stalling and telling lies, he had to confess that he never had one. No need for it in the past. He was fired in spite of his years of service and untainted record.

The local authorities were also checking and double-checking taxi-drivers' papers. A strange action, to say the least; for, that was one occupation open to any qualified person and the only qualifications required were a driving permit and knowledge of the city. Of course, his African intelligence helped him to learn all the names of the streets, and the confusing nooks and corners, in record time. And he had a driving permit. His taxi was his own personal vehicle painted in black and white, with a caption on its side, *Destiny Cab Co.* News spread that special permits were being introduced for foreigners driving or owning a taxi. Any offender was liable to become an unwilling guest of the federal government. He was therefore constrained to reduce his presence on the road.

The abrupt change from an open society to a repressive one, was brought about by many factors. Each person whom he knew, had an explanation for it. But he was convinced that his own opinion was nearest to the truth: Too many Africans were flooding the Great Society, or God's own country. He hoped and prayed that some of them would be repatriated.

In those days when only reasonable, aspiring young men used to come to America, there were no difficulties at all. He himself used to know every other compatriot living in that gigantic city. There was love among them all, and everyone was prepared to be his brother's keeper. Besides, they were law-abiding citizens. Nonetheless, with the influx of hot-headed and irresponsible elements -and he was tempted to believe that all newcomers, that is, all those coming after him, belonged in that category- distrust and denigration of the race set in. With his latest difficulties, he was compelled to abhor those boisterous, Greek-spitting Africans crowding the subway, buses, and commercial center. Their faces always stood out in the crowd. Moon faces. Black faces. Ugly faces! They were forever shouting at the top of their voices, in that strange language that he could no longer understand. How ashamed he was to have originated from the same land as those fools! His tailoring business had lost its heavy impact and flow of dollars, simply because those JJCs made dashikis too common. In addition, their disgraceful behavior turned off the soul brothers and sisters from their spiritual quest for the ancestral home. Finally, the rash of arrests of providers of instantaneous happiness through the paradisiacal smoke of marijuana, had slowed down his grass business.

He had to act fast, or else... His phone rang.

"Hello."

"Hi, baby. What's new?"

"Who's speaking?"

"It's me, of course, your sweet Mona Lisa, who else could it be, man?"

"Just jiving, just jiving. I knew it was you the very instant the phone rang. So what's up?"

"Ain't nothing much, honey. Want me to come over tonight?"

"Oh, I'm sorry, I've got things to do, something real important to take care of."

"Know what? I suspect you jungle nigger's two-timing me. You got yourself another mama, right? But I'm warning you now, I'll mess up her ass if I ever lay my hands on her!"

"Come on, Lisa baby, there ain't no one but you. I only have to do some work on my research project at the college."

"Yeah, all you Africans, always working, studying, doing all them white stuff! But that's why I loved you the moment I met you. You all ain't like our guys here; no school, no job, no responsibility. When are you gonna finish college, anyway?"

"Soon, baby, pretty soon, if only you give me a chance to do some work..."

"All right, sugar, make sure you call me when you get back home tonight, no matter how late, OK?"

"Of course, baby, I will. Take care now, and see you."

He sighed heavily.

Mona Lisa, she was something else. Black and beautiful. Long, shining hair. Firm figure. Rich family. Understanding, very understanding. She did not go to college, but was bent upon marrying a college-trained man, preferably an African with no plans to return home. He was that African.

If he asked her for financial help, she should gladly oblige, but he could not. The son of a rich African tycoon and king should never need money...

Time was running out. He picked up his princess telephone and touched the number of a friend from the old days. The latter had continued to do well, amassing not only dollars but academic qualifications. Unlike the tailor, he had left home with the necessary qualifications for college admission and had made good use of his educational opportunities. Both men were agreed on one important point: no use returning home to Africa.

"Hello."

"Hi, is that you, old boy?"

"Yeah, it's me! Eh, what's happening? Hope your problems are now over."

"Not really. In fact, that's why I'm calling you. Could I see you some time this evening? There is something urgent I'd like you to help me with."

"Um, well, you see, I'm a little busy right now. But, I mean, OK, you may come over. I have to go on a date, but I shall cancel it, just for you... Things are so tight these days."

"Thanks a lot, thanks a lot! Expect me then around seven. Bye."

"All right, bye."

It was a brief visit. He had everything well planned beforehand and, of course, once assured of success, his friend agreed to help see it through.

"Man must wack o!" one said to the other boisterously. They hit each other playfully and laughed in jubilation. They jumped into their respective cars and drove off towards downtown. The two drivers, surrounded by a crowd of onlookers, were engaged in a vehement argument when the police arrived on the scene of the pre-planned accident. The two vehicles had run into each other front against rear, and the driver of the vehicle in front was complaining very loudly of a whiplash, various forms of headache, and all sorts of body-aches. The second driver kept shouting something about unnecessary use of brakes and lack of driving ability. He was making deliberately unsuccessful attempts to get at his victim. The policeman kept holding him off, while telling him to be calm and reasonable, that the other driver was hurt and might collapse under any attack.

The policeman, visibly disgusted with the whole scene, took their particulars, especially the insurance policy numbers. Both men happened to be using the same company. The company's representative would naturally clear the mess; meanwhile, the police quickly cleared the road.

With visits to the doctor who would support the claims of assorted aches and pains, the cunning ex-tailor figured on a heavy financial claim from the insurance company. He also retained a reputable insurance claims attorney who assured him that, the longer the sickness, the better for all those concerned.

Days of expectation. Elaborate plans for the imminent windfall. Dollars spent in dreams. He could hardly wait to feel the real greenbacks in his hands. Visits to the famous neighborhood men's wear store to verify prices of clothes at which he could only steal glances in the past. Deposit on a color television set similar to the one he had seen at the mansion of Mona's father. He had long, sleepless nights, and enjoyed every minute of them.

While waiting for the green fortune, he decided, much against his will, to take some money from his loving Mona Lisa, and promised to pay her back when his allowance arrived from his royalty of a dad. She knew foreign exchange was always difficult to obtain in those African countries and that her darling had managed to beat the archaic bureaucracy through his father's influence. According to him, things were lately becoming rather more difficult than before. Indeed, Lisa would have no part of any payback, never. For once in their relationship, she had the occasion to dent his ego, and that elated her.

A short wait became a long, agonizing one. Month came after month, and still no check was in the mail. The patient had to overcome his illness, but his pockets were still sick with emptiness.

At last, he received a letter from the insurance company asking him and his friend to call at the representative's office to sign some important papers about the approved claims. He jumped so high, his head almost hit the ceiling.

The kind doctor was to take one-eighth of the loot; the understanding attorney, another eighth. The friends would share the rest, although the question of percentage was not discussed. One thing was taken for granted: Personal needs and the origin of the great idea, would be given due consideration.

At the insurance agent's office, there were two gentlemen -company trainees in client affairs, they were called- sitting in on the meeting with the representative. The latter congratulated the two honest policy-holders for their forthrightness and good fortune. They were fortunate to be alive and should be more careful in future, especially the one who hit his brother from behind. The documents were duly signed and, jocularly, the agent said something about brothers running into each other's car so often that one might wonder whether Providence was not playing tricks on people. He used to work in Africa, and was wondering whether the duo came from the same country.

"Yes, of course," beamed the ex-tailor. "We actually came over here the same year. Our families live only a couple of streets apart back home and, unlike many others who came after us, we have worked hard and retained our customarily strong ties, and self-pride, and dignity, and..."

Everybody laughed heartily, particularly the client affairs' trainees. Then, suddenly, a metallic object flashed across his face, followed by the words:

"FBI. We'd like to ask you both a few questions."

He spent the night in jail. His friend, too, in another cell. The latter was released the following morning. Mr. Quick-Head-Fast-Mouth had no one to bail him out. He instructed his friend not to tell Mona Lisa about the incident, thus leaving it up to the accomplice alone to find the necessary funds for bail.

Trust quickly became a thing of the past, and much more so as it involved hard cash. Nobody was expected to be broke in the land of plenty, particularly African princes and children of tycoons.

One day, many weeks later, they found his body hanging from the ceiling of his cell.

Wives, Lovers and Intellectuals

"Hello, hello, operator, hello, hello..."

"Yees, hello, wetin una want? Gently, gently now, you dey break my eardrum o!"

"Yeah, darling dear, those nasty boys at your office, na wa o. They just don't seem to understand that you are the boss and therefore deserve all the respect in the world..."

"Hello, hello, operator, can you hear me, can you hear me?!!!"

"For example, the other day, when I called on you during my lunch-break, your stupid messenger, I am sure he was acting in collusion with the secretary, he told me you were in a conference. I told the idiot that you, darling, were expecting me."

"Don't worry about all those asses working under me, Nana, I know how to handle them all. But the point is this: Maybe it is not very wise for you to come around that often. We see a lot of each other outside office hours, after all, and..."

"Wetin be de matter wit dis man? Don't shout, I tell you, DON'T SHOUT!!! Anyway, wu do you want, wat numbah are you calling?"

"Operator, I am trying to get 222216, but the line does not seem to be working."

"Wat do you mean de line is not walking? All lines are walking, you ear, all lines ear walk!!!"

"... There is not much we can do in the office."

"Darling, you don't seem to understand that seeing in itself is doing, sometimes. My day at Establishments will be totally, absolutely, boring if I don't see your pretty face. Your presence makes my day, and there's not much I can do work-wise if I don't see you. Indeed, I look forward to seeing you during breaks, and that gives my day a meaning, it makes it so much shorter."

"OK, mister man, your line is true now, go a'ead and stop bodering me."

"Thanks a lot, miss. Hello, is that Tunji?"

"Yes, how are things, Ade? What have you been doing with your good self? I've not seen you in quite a while."

"Things have been a bit rough. Boy, this our telephone system makes me sick! You can't imagine how hard it was for me to get through to you. I even thought of going across to see you personally, only I'm waiting for someone here. And the operator..."

"Well, dear, maybe we'll have to work out something else. I've been thinking, I could try to move you to our office here. I know some under-secretaries are resigning to go into private business and, possibly, just possibly, we could have you shifted to fill one of the positions. I'll send out feelers and let you know the outcome."

"Oh, darling, darling, I know that you really love me. I wish I could see you right now to plant a big kiss on your lips. My make-up and lip-stick would have been messed up, but it would have been worth the trouble. All the same, here is a big one for you. I am sending it across the line this very minute. Ready?"

"Well, I'm calling you about the forthcoming conference on the Relevance of National Languages to African Independence and the Valuation and Dissemination of African Culture and Civilization. You know it's being held in the States a month from now and, of course, I'd love to go."

"Yeah, I have the papers on my desk, somewhere. But I never thought you were interested in this language stuff. No matter how you look at it, the European languages, particularly English and French, have helped immensely in the modernization of a major part of this continent and, to all intents and purposes, they now constitute national languages of Africa."

"I agree with you to a certain extent but, to my mind, all avenues for the improvement of the impact of our African languages are worth exploring. We appear to forget many times that our greatest philosophers and historical figures did not know a single word of these foreign languages."

"OK, darling, when am I going to see you next?"

"I don't know. I really don't know. You see, I was going to send a messenger with a note to you, but I never got around to writing it. I've been busy."

"A note? Why write a note when all you have to do is ask and I'll come streaking to the rendezvous? Henry, don't be funny, you dirty old man. Or, are you mad at me for not giving it to you the last time? You know I was sick and when I'm sick, it is just not worth doing."

"That is not it, dear, that's not it at all. But there are some sacrifices I've been making, willingly, mind you, that are backfiring on me, so to speak."

"Talk of sacrifices! Not seeing you on any given day, allowing you to go back and sleep on the same bed with that illiterate that you call wife, isn't that the greatest sacrifice that I, or anyone else for that matter, could ever make? Tell me, how many people in this country..."

"Operator, operator!!!"

"Dis people are craassy o! Wat do dey all want?"

"... in this world, can condone what I have been putting up with?"

"Mama Iyabo, you have come again o, don't you know all men are the same?"

"I don't know about all men, I only know about Daddy. He is very responsible, very kind, very human, very everything. He treats all his children and me as he should, he meets all our needs and never runs around. I can assure you that I have complete trust in Daddy."

"Come on, man, stop all this preaching about languages which are actually irrelevant to progress in these modern times. Whether we like it or not, modern technology and civilization are here to stay, and meetings held in every capital on earth about the valuation of African languages will not change that. Modern destiny is the only viable one for Africa, and you and I had better realize that before it is too late. Now, if you still wish to go to that nonsensical conference..."

"Eeeh, Mama Iyabo, you really trust your husband, and I really envy you. But, let me tell you, don't be too sure that there is nothing on the side. These smart secretaries these days are to be feared o. I am not saying that my husband does..."

"So, what are you saying then? If you know that your husband can be trusted, why can't I trust mine? Maybe your man even has something to hide!"

"I have not said my husband can, or cannot, be trusted; that is not the point. Your own man is more in the public eye than mine, and that is always a great danger."

"I don't see any danger in being successful. Besides, you can be sure that I am not talking for nothing. Everyone has to take precautions. Daddy eats at home, regularly, and that is enough already."

"Ah, now I get your point. I shall call on you soon and you can teach me a few things about..."

"Oh, no, I am not going to teach you anything! You are the confident one and, as far as I am concerned, you don't need anybody's help. Least of all mine. You should be quite satisfied."

"I must set the record straight, Tunji. I am not saying that Africa should lag behind in technological know-how. My contention is, that we must do something to preserve our own culture and, as you well know, language is a major part of culture."

"What is the big deal about these languages, anyway? You and I never had to learn our language at school, and we did pretty well. Still, we can read any text, or almost any, written in our language quite well, which is all we need."

"But, I think there is more to it. I personally feel embarrassed when I speak our language to someone and I have to mix it with foreign words, just because I don't know the correct word in our language."

"So, you need some lessons in the local terminologies. But to attend a conference in faraway America to do that..."

"Oh, no, that is not the whole point. You know one needs to get away once in a while, to keep one's sanity in this place, as you yourself used to say, remember? Moreover, I have not returned to the States in a while, and I really should. I have some things to take care of over there."

"Ah, there. You should have said that much earlier, instead of propounding all those theories about values of primitive dialects."

"Well, darling, what sacrifices are you talking about?"

"Let me see, you know there are gossips all over the place, wicked tongues always prepared to smear one's good name, especially when they know one is successful."

"So, Mama Iyabo, you refuse to help a friend, hein? Anyway, your extraordinary precautions notwithstanding, I still feel you should watch your husband very closely, like any other woman has to, and does."

"You have to watch your own husband!!! Let us change the subject, please!!! How are your children doing at their new school?"

"They are doing very well, thank God. Their poor father, he seems preoccupied these days, and I think it has to do with that mate of his getting promoted to the post of Senior Lecturer. I wish I could help him. These days one can't trust anybody, I tell you. Our universities don't place any emphasis on work. My poor Ade, he has no long legs, and I wish he could find a way."

"Well, well, so you have a problem at your place. Who would have believed that? I thought everything was rolling along perfectly for you."

"Tunji, you know I need that trip extremely urgently. Linda wrote the other day and mentioned the sad condition she and our kid are in. More and more, things are becoming very hard to bear. I am ashamed of all the lies I've been telling to both sides."

"But, man, you've got to be very careful, very very careful!!! You must handle these things like a man. You can't allow yourself to be fooled by a woman's emotionalism. Linda is doing her own thing over there, I am sure, and I thought you gave up that kid once you decided to return home."

"Don't get me wrong now. I am not planning to do anything drastic. My family is right here at home. But one cannot simply forget a part of one's self, as if it never existed. Imagine my irresponsibility, giving up a child, my very first child, my son!!!"

"All right, Ade, the trip is yours for the taking. You did not expect me to refuse your request, did you? After all, we've been friends for ages."

"Thanks a lot, buddy, thanks a lot."

"Darling, you are getting scared of your wife, isn't that the plain truth?"

"Oh, no, impossible! How could I? She's a gentle, sedentary, retiring woman, a perfect mother for my children."

"Yes, I know she is a great homebody, but I also know that she is feared by many many young ladies in this city. They have told me how much power she possesses, but I just don't care about all that. In England..."

"What! What! What happened in England? Don't tell me you were fooling around in London!"

"Darling dear, I was only going to tell you what happened to a friend of mine over there. Nothing to do with me, nothing at all. Anyway, you have still not pinpointed those sacrifices of yours."

"Perhaps we should let sleeping dogs lie. Nothing has been revealed for sure and, as I've said, I shall send out feelers about your

39

move to our main office, maybe on secondment, or something."

"Well, honey, I'm looking forward to our next physical communication. Oh, I just can't wait..."

"What is happening on this stupid line? There are all sorts of weird things going on with the phones in this crazy country!"

"What do you mean? I can hear you perfectly well on this side."

"If I am not mistaken, that is my wife's voice on the line. I can hear her very very clearly!!!"

"Your wife's voice? I think you are daydreaming, I mean, overwhelmed by thoughts of your charming Lande."

"No kidding, it is *her* voice!!!"

"Hello, hello, hello! Operator, this damn line is going bananas... Are you still there?"

"Mama Iyabo, can you hear me, can you hear me now?"

"Darling dear, I am really looking forward to that rendezvous. Let's go to Hilton-Africa next. Tonight? How about tonight?"

"Sorry, dear, I have to take the family to my colleague's place. One of his children is celebrating his birthday and my wife is seizing the opportunity to return a visit paid us by their family some time ago."

"What a life!!!"

"Mama Iyabo, hello, hello, what is happening again to this line!!!"

"You know, I'm starting to hear voices. There is Daddy talking to a lady with a seductive voice. Just to arouse my jealousy, he is putting her on the run, he is making her feel that he loves her. That stupid brat, she is going to get it from me! This means that some nasty woman is trying to snatch Daddy away from me and the children. I have to go now and work on something. I shall be talking to you again soon. And, thank you for calling; your unfounded fears have been very helpful. The spirits have talked to me, and I must act at once. Perhaps..."

"Darling, honey, darling, I can't hear you anymore. Operator, operator, operator!!! You had better reconnect me, or I shall have you fired, you incompetent imp!!! Don't you know who I am?"

"Mama Iyabo, what is going on? Are you still there? I need that thing badly, please. Are you..."

"Lande? Could it be..."

"Mama..."

"Eh, man, stop..."

"Operator, could you kindly get me this number:

40

2220000000000000000000?"

"What?!!!"

"Are you mad?"

A loud voice roared in mocking laughter over the telephone, recently repaired at an unannounced cost of fifty billion africa, by a trio of companies from America, Britain, and Canada.

Then, suddenly, all the lines went completely dead, perhaps temporarily, perhaps forever.

A Slice of Life

The life of a hero at National Secondary School, Apata-Ganga, Wafrica: Unsanctioned privileges, the adulation of innumerable fans, the camaraderie of mates aspiring to his level of flagrant disregard for regulations, the ire of the Headmaster and his obsequious staff. The life of a revered outlaw.

Akaraogun just lived the life. He did not love it. He did not hate it. He simply lived it to the hilt.

He excelled in everything he did, with amazing ease. He successfully combined academics with pleasure much to the dismay and displeasure of the vast majority of the college community.

"Aakara... Akara... Ogun... Ogun..."

"Eh... eeh... eeeh... eeeeh..."

"One... two... three... it's a goal!!! Aaakaaaraaaa!!!"

The crowd at the football matches came to see him dazzle them with his footwork. He would pick up the ball with his left foot, flip it onto the right, and gracefully meander his way through a crowd of opposing players. It all happened so effortlessly that many were those that honestly believed that he was born with a ball glued to his feet. Others vowed that he was some sort of wizard blessed with superhuman powers by his witch of a grandmother. It was his penultimate year at the secondary school. Before each match, they all stood up and sang in unison about their hero's artistry. Arguments and predictions of his imminent feat often led to blows among friends.

"Today na goal galore!"

"Ow many goal, you tink?"

"Ma fren, man no dey ass sush keston. Wen we say gol, we mean gol... gol galore. Na basket dey go take pack am go dem dety school, dis *ayo* people."

"Eh, you sef, wetin you dey talk your mout dey sweet so as if una dey wan kech buttocks of a woman wey dey pass? I say, Akara go score

43

four gol today."

"Stupid nonsense! Shut up your gutter of a mout!!! When man talk monkey listen, you ere? We who mattah don see all Akara games for dis college, and all na goal galore. Dis words pass your woman understandin."

Once the match started, opposing teams quickly lost their composure after his first waltz through their porous defense. The outcome of the game was predictable: Victory for Akaraogun's team.

The ensuing jubilation went beyond human understanding. The diminutive hero, carried on the shoulders of human horses, rode the waves of adulation right up to his dormitory. The feet of kings never touch the ground. Angels soar like birds above mere mortals. Akaraogun will live forever. Some tore off his soaked jersey as souvenir of another memorable match. Others tried desperately, in vain, to touch the shining, ebony skin, while others still simply stared, mouths agape, waiting for the buzz of Wafrica's giant flies to put a bolt on their toothy holes. The short period was as long as the life time of an octogenarian. The experience was as full of variety as the lived experience of a woman of easy virtues.

Only Akaraogun, the bond between brothers with no link but the blood coursing through their veins, the hero unaware of the uniqueness of his unequalled feats, kept his composure, as usual, with ease. He was tired, and the only thought that sneaked through his mind was of the film currently playing at the Roxy Theatre: A young rebel, without love, with much love for life, leaves his village home for the city. Enrolled in the Government High School, he meets a beautiful girl, falls madly in love with her, but with no reciprocity on her part. He is, however, convinced that she loves him. He plans to marry and take her back to the village. One warm night, she confesses that she hardly loves him, that she is only fascinated by his intelligence and rebellious nature, and that she is not ready to settle down...

"Akaraogun is great!"

"But how great can you be when you cannot follow orders and abide by society's laws?"

"Come on, you are just jealous of the young man. Let us face it, he's one in a million. You know, I, too, played some sports in my secondary school days. Only, I could never combine that with booking."

"Well, well, that's life."

44

His critics on the staff blamed the Headmaster for giving him too much freedom. Some believed that the young man should have been suspended for violating college regulations, while others were convinced that he was a bad influence on the junior students. But Mr. Bullock, an enterprising expatriate very much committed to the reputation of his school, disagreed with his subordinates. In his opinion, Akaraogun was a rare breed, an exceptional talent that needed to be understood. The good in him outweighed the evil, and the school could not afford to lose him. Mr. Bullock therefore went out of his way to treat the popular hero with gentleness. He cajoled him, he overlooked his many misdemeanors, and always defended him before those who were out to expel him from the institution.

One difficulty stood in the Headmaster's way: Akaraogun himself. He could not care less what Mr. Bullock, or anyone else, thought or did. He just lived his life. No questions asked; none answered.

Part of the Headmaster's plan for the boy's final year at school was to give him a position of responsibility. He announced to the staff the decision to make Akaraogun the captain of football. The all-African staff grumbled in near unison, but none of them had the courage to question the master's decision. Contrary to protocol, Mr. Bullock sent for Akaraogun the evening preceding the assembly honoring the school's new student leaders. He informed the boy over a tall glass of coca-cola, that he was to become the football captain, a great honor which would enhance his already high standing in the community.

Akaraogun simply set another record in the school's annals: He became the first student of the famous National High School of Wafrica, to turn down such an honor. The Headmaster and his staff were stunned. Some fellow students, upon learning of the secret, applauded the hero's defiance of authority and the younger ones, in particular, loved him more than ever before. Many questions were raised by the boy's unusual action and, years after his departure from the school, many still wondered why he had refused an opportunity to lead, to use his God-given power to shape the destiny of a whole, young community.

Rumor had it that Mr. Bullock planned to expel him outright from the school, but nothing happened. The Headmaster had another interview with his rebel of a hero who asserted that it was against his family's tradition to take a role of leadership. He said his brother was once a school prefect and the whole experience was disastrous. He would not explain further, however.

The headmaster kept that strange story to himself. He would not divulge it to anybody, in spite of the negative rumors flying all over the school.

"You should try to understand the lad," the man used to say in the staff room, to no one in particular. No one could.

Akaraogun continued to perform brilliantly at school and on the sports field. His anti-establishment posture did not slow down either. He never missed a popular film in town. His bevy of beauties in nearby secondary schools was always at hand whenever he attended a party. He left the school premises at will, never with permission, any day of the week, and any hour of the day.

The day of the final game of the football season was a Saturday. The hero got up early and left for downtown in a hurry. His number one girl was waiting for him at the United African Foodmart, Limited, for the usual breakfast of donuts and coffee. She was looking radiant in her well-ironed and starched blue and white uniform. Her black skin was shining under the tropical morning sun. Akaraogun was sitting there acknowledging greetings of anonymous fans. His school blazer was thrown carelessly over his shoulders. His girl tried to rush him through the breakfast. She did not wish to share him with all those hounds prowling in the store. They soon jumped into a taxi and headed for her sister's house. The same empty, two-bedroom bungalow abandoned during weekends by a family that must return to their village for traditional reunions. The same queen-sized bed. The same two bodies communicating feverishly, greedily, and heartily. The same sweet nothings whispered by teenage lips into teenage ears. The same slice of life jammed into a few stolen moments. The same fire kindled every weekend. The same ecstasy lived out by two ignorant souls.

Akaraogun became exhausted rather quickly. He pushed his partner, or victim, away with a little sign of disgust, and soon fell fast asleep, snoring like a drunk. As usual, the girl was overjoyed just to be lying there by the hero's side. She would not mind at all, even if he decided to beat her like a raging lover. Just to be with him, just being with him, was worth anything. He got up after a while, washed his snaring face, in a rush, threw an indifferent good-bye at her, and headed back to school. She would follow later, because she must see the big game.

Back at school, a car pulled up at the iron gate and, after a series of questions and answers, the driver was allowed to enter. He made for the hero's hall of residence. A lady sat quietly at the back of the small vehicle. She instructed the young, uniformed driver to enter the building and ask for Akaraogun. He was not yet back from town.

They would have to wait. The Hall Master was informed of the lady's presence. He came to the vehicle and invited her into his house nearby, to wait for her absent brother. His wife could prepare something for her and the driver. She refused to move. She sat there, quietly, at the back of the car. She soon dozed off, then woke up, staring at nothing, something, or everything.

The hero returned about an hour before game time. He was feeling very good, after stopping for a couple of hours to eat and relax at his second girl-friend's house. He was ready for his final game as the school's hero. He would take a shower and then go to the field to warm up and loosen up. The arena of his past, present, and permanent glory was waiting for him. His fans, forever faithful and fanatical, were already converging on the arena.

Just before he went into the shower, a friend informed him of the lady sitting in the car. He ran out, wondering what his sister could be doing there, some two hundred miles away from the family home. He did not have a second to concoct a story about his absence from the residence. No need for any stories, when the reality of life strikes.

"You have to come home with me, Akara. Olu is sick, and Papa says we should all gather together to perform some important rituals."

Olu was his immediate senior brother, the one whose name he had used to tell that famous lie to the headmaster. For once in his illustrious career, Akaraogun ran the risk of missing a football match, and his final one at that. His thoughts went to his brother.

But, Olu cannot be ill. He is as strong as a bull, he is resilient, tough, unconquerable. He has never been ill, so he cannot be ill now. And, you cannot miss the last game of your great career, just like that, for reasons no better than glorified speculation. Olu, Olu is so alive, so full of vigor, he cannot be sick...

The hero never played that last match, or any other, in the arena of his last glory, or in any other arena of life. A few miles from home, the driver ran into a long petrol tanker. Akaraogun's sister died instantly. The driver escaped with minor injury, and the hero had multiple fracture of both feet, and a broken spinal cord. The driver panicked. As soon as he had freed himself from the twisted, burning metal, he took to his heels, darting around stumps and trees, warding off offending branches with his hands of steel, and mumbling incoherently to himself.

Perhaps madam is safe back home, carried there by the wind... It is surprising that the special beads made by the village medicine man did not prevent the accident... What will oga say when he learns of this new mishap, after the death of his son? ... And, young master, is he alive, or dead, too?... Heaven forbid o, my mother has always told me, don't go back, never go back to the scene of an accident. Run, run, run!!!

Akaraogun lay there helpless, for the very first, and last, time in his heroic life. Unable to move a muscle, he could only watch as the flames were chewing up the wrecked metal, and the body of his dear, dead sister. The fire was now approaching him, slowly but surely. He began to scream to the desert of death and despair. Help was a world away, refusing to come, bent upon taking its time, until tomorrow which would never come in time.

A couple of days later, surveyors working on the ultra-modern, already pot-holed national expressway saw the charred carcasses of man and metal disturbing their patriotic, and progressive work. One worker nonchalantly raked aside the stinking mess with his boots while another, very considerate, covered the still visible plate-number of the vehicle with his dirty handkerchief. Nothing must stop the process of modernization.

Windfall

The news on the national radio was clear, and the reader was deliberate, with a tinge of irony in his mellifluous voice:

"The government of the Federal Republic today announced a wage increase for all public servants."

Officer Oba was sitting cozily in his police cruiser when he heard the news. His heart almost jumped out of his body. He was excited, he was shaking all over with joy, he couldn't wait to get home and talk to his wife about his plans for the new money.

"Lord, that cannot be true! Impossible! So, at last, at long last, I can buy my motorbike. At last...," he sighed.

On the other side of town, Daddy Alao, a Senior Clerk with over forty years' experience on the job, had just finished listening to the 12 o'clock report on his pint-sized transistor set. Tears welled in his eyes. He did not make any effort to hold them back, even though he knew that his junior workers were crowded round the radio. He was not ashamed to cry; for, how better to end his days in the service of the nation, than with a hundred per cent increase in his salary? The new government had expressed its commitment to providing the needs of the commoners, and he had often said exactly the same thing to his co-workers, and his wife, and his children. With the new law, every employee would be able to live, instead of merely existing.

Daddy's mind raced through the years, back to his earliest days as a Class Four graduate employed as a clerical officer in his home town. How proud he was! His father and mother, God bless their departed souls, used to parade him every Sunday at church, presenting him to their friends as their *oyinbo*, that is, a white man. He could have blushed if he had been white! But he was inwardly elated to be so highly respected by family and friends alike. By obtaining his Class Four diploma, he had reached the pinnacle of academic excellence. There was no holding him back. Once employed in the district office, his eyes were set on attaining another high rung: his own desk and chair at the national Secretariat in the capital.

The journey to the top was rough. He lost his parents soon after graduation, and his first wife and two children also passed away. Nonetheless, he was not discouraged. He just lived out his destiny, never doubting the Almighty's plans for him. His transfer to the capital was abrupt, and there were still a few individuals back home who thought he had either used some black magic, or bribed his way out of the regional office. The note from the District Officer was terse: "You are being transferred to the national Secretariat effective a week from today. Good luck."

So, there he was at the capital, first sharing a desk with three other employees, but finally having his own desk.

Daddy's comportment and attire hardly changed over the years: Always calm and collected with barely a smile hidden at the left corner of his mouth, he donned a white suit with a white shirt to match, brown tie and shoes, and a white helmet that he removed only indoors. The helmet was given to him by an old District Officer for whom he used to run errands back in his home town. He acquired his nickname from his first days at the district office. A colleague looked at him fixedly, shook his head, smiled, and called him "Daddy."

"What do you mean by dat? I am only twenty!"

"Ah, ah, dat's what we all say. Even when we are fifty, we still like to call ourselves twenty! Just like me, I have three different ages: one for my school records, one for my job and, of course, one for my family who are not even sure which is which."

"I don't care! I know I am twenty, and dat's de trut."

"Anyway, don't be annoyed, I call you Daddy because your suit and helmet are very special. When you came in just now, you reminded me of my fader in his days as a Senior Clerk. His helmet was given to him by a colonial officer. Your own looks so much like his."

The nickname stuck. As the years passed by, Daddy, too, came to cultivate some liking for it. Many younger elements used it to address him, as a sign of respect, and who would refuse to be respected? No doubt, others saw in him the symbol of a dead period, particularly since the style of his suit did not evolve with the times. All the same, every new employee was sent to his room to see neatness in person, so as to aspire to such heights later in the service. The road to Daddy's room was always overcrowded. Apart from the heavy turnover of employees, which naturally increased the number of seekers of the epitome of neatness, there was a growing following for Daddy's wisdom and expertise in public service regulations. *General Orders*, G.O., in popular office language, an old fat book filled with every article of public service rules, was kept under lock and key in Daddy's office, and the symbol of decorum and discipline knew just about all the articles in the text.

"According to section 47 sub-section C regulation 27 paragraph 5, every officer appointed at the level of Clerk Grade II is eligible for a 10% increase after two years of service."

" Daddy, Daddy, I knew you would not fail me, I just knew it! Now I can go to my Head of Division and tell him to recommend me."

Daddy was brought back to reality by a wild laughter from across the room. He literally stood up from his seat.

"Hein, hein, did someone say someting?"

"No," replied Oye, his immediate junior officer. "Daddy, you appeared to be dreaming. You were crying, too. Hope nothing?"

"Oh, no, not at all. Were you not listening to de radio? De government, I told you boys dis is de greatest government ever, dey are giving all of us a big raise. A hundred per cent raise! Double salary from now on! What a way to reward me for all dese years! If you saw tears in my eyes, Oye, it is tears of joy, you really cannot understand... You cannot understand at all at all!"

"But, Daddy," shot out another voice, "you are making a big mistake o! I tell you, this government is not better than the rest of them. You will see, all the cash money you are weeping about, is already being eyed by our greedy merchants and market women."

Everyone in the room became suddenly silent. The speaker was the latest arrival at the office. His full name was Smart Babington Alexander, but people called him *Smarty*, or *The Great*. A Higher School Certificate holder, he succeeded rather quickly in alienating himself from both his colleagues and superiors.

"I am only here to while away the time," he used to tell whoever cared to listen. "I'm going to the States come September, so I don't give a damn about this stupid place."

Such pomposity could not but arouse the ire of most of the other workers. For many, the Secretariat was a dead end, and the Civil

Service a terminal case of cancer. Their job constituted a point of no return. Theirs was to be a long life of waking up at six in the morning, washing up, choking themselves with a tie, and slowly dropping into their faded woolen suits. At the office, they would look at the same files, and see the same tired faces, like reflections in a many-sided mirror. If they left the Secretariat, it would only be to return to the regional office, a setback not happily anticipated by any of them. Many abhorred the monotonous ride in the over-crowded, capricious buses taking them to and from work. They detested even more the long, uneventful hours inside the office where they had to fight for space with files, flies, and cockroaches. But the alternative to all that was to stay at home. Home was hell, with the wife always nagging about the lack of funds, the emaciated children staring you in the face and asking unspoken questions, and the boredom and nothingness populating the whole diseased atmosphere. It was, indeed, a most welcome event when dawn showed its happy, but sad face, cutting short the night filled with its hallucinations and endless discussions with the wife, and of a non-existent future.

Smarty was naturally the latest of the many ills that awaited the workers at Daddy's office. Down to the last messenger, they all tried their best to accommodate the braggart. They pretended not to listen to his harsh remarks, but it was always apparent that their pretext, their silence, was a hollow mask concealing their eagerness to have him explain himself further, and their guilt that whatever he said had a ring of truth to it. They could not ignore what the young man had to say. Daddy had once advised them in Smarty's absence to desist from having any confrontation with him. "Silence," said the wise old man, "is de best answer for a fool."

This time, it was Daddy himself who was guilty of answering a fool.

"Smarty, just shut up and try to listen to what we are telling you!"

"Daddy, it's you that should see with me, because I know, and you know, that I am right, as usual. As I was saying before I was rudely interrupted, all this money is only going to cause trouble for everybody."

"All right, Smart Head, let me ask you sometin. Which government before now has done anytin for de common man of dis nation?"

"None, absolutely none! But my contention is, that this one's offer of an increment in salaries is nothing but a political game."

52

"Well, politics or no politics, I assure you dat dis increase is de best tin dat has happened to us in a long time. You young men of today, you just have no respect for your elders. Some of you always tink dat you know everytin. You will see, just be patient, just keep listening to de radio, and you will see."

Oye whispered something to one of those sitting near Daddy's desk. Then, he shouted out at Smarty:

"Why don't you go to your America, and stop being stupid!!!"

Smarty pretended not to hear. He started to hum a song, turned on his heels, and swaggered out of the room, his hands stuck in his hip pockets. Oye could only hiss loudly after him.

Officer Oba was on his way back home after a long day. But the new money had eradicated from his mind all the usual thoughts of boredom and fatigue. He rode his Raleigh bicycle unusually fast that evening.

"Hello, captain."

"Oga sah, how you dey dis even?"

"Esis sah, mah broda say he dey come see una tonite o."

The greetings and messages went on and on, as Officer Oba, a veritable Very Important Personality in the neighborhood, sped down the street toward his one-bedroom flat.

Sola was waiting at the verandah, as usual. She knew exactly when her man would ride up to the door. After preparing his meal and setting the table, she would go and take a bath, change into something attractive -revealing would be a more appropriate word- and take her place on the chair outside.

She was yet to hear the good news about the new money.

Officer Oba reached home. He turned the corner with a flurry. He let his left foot drop to ground-level, bent his body and the front of the machine to the left and put on the brakes ever so slightly. The booted foot dragged along the ground, raising a cloud of dust on the untarred road. He rang the bell of his machine three times before coming to a screeching stop.

Sola jumped upon him with glee.

"Darling, I have missed you all day long."

He gave her a smile filled with self-satisfaction and replied, "I know, I know... Did you hear the good news?"

"Which good news, which one again, o? *Abi* you have been promoted? Are they giving you another rope? Oh, I shall be so glad, I shall tell all my friends."

"No, no, no! But you really don't know, hein? Come in and let me tell you inside... I don't want you to be over-excited now. Just sit down quietly and let me tell you."

He went in and ran out again. He went back in, and back out. He repeated the action three times, while advising his wife to keep calm.

"Darling, tell me now. What is this news you are keeping from me so? Why is it so hard for you to stay in one place and tell me? Tell me now, I beg."

"All right, listen to this... OK, let me tell you right now... Here we go... You won't believe this... My salary is going to be... is going to be... has been... doubled. Doubled!!! I tell you, two times what I have been collecting until now!!!"

Sola almost hit the roof. She knocked over the loudspeaker next to her chair and tried hard to set it back upright.

"Eh, eh, na wa o. My dear husby, na wa! God don do us sometin big, big, big!!! *Oluwa o!* What shall we do with all that money? No, I need some new dresses, and I told you that Patty's getting married soon, and Esther's granny died last week. We should start thinking of a baby, too. And remember Henrietta? She went to London on business only two days ago; I will like to go soon myself. After all, she does not even have a husband..."

"Sola, we have to think seriously of what to do with this windfall. We must be composed because such an opportunity comes only once in a lifetime. I think the new money will start this month, which is only a few days away. At the station, the Superintendent told me that the whole thing will be retroactive by six months."

"Eeh, eh! Don't tell me your English has changed already. You cannot even wait for us to have the windfall in our hands before you start throwing heavy English at me. I have never heard that word before, not in England, or elsewhere. Retrospective, that is one nice English."

"Darling, I said, re-tro-active."

"Retractive, what does it mean?"

Officer Oba could not sleep a wink that night. His head was heavy with plans, money plans. The least of his worries was Sola who was fast asleep by his side. She had ridden his coat-tail to fame and fortune. He married her a year before, on one of those infrequent journeys back to his village. She was fresh out of modern school, a not-too-bright student, but generally acclaimed as the most beautiful girl in the whole village of some five hundred people. His mother had suggested that he visit Sola's father, a local chief blessed with many wives and innumerable children.

"Oh, captain, welcome, welcome, you are welcome. My house is your house. How is the capital?"

"All right, sir, all right. And how about your health? I hope my mothers and sisters are looking after you very well?"

"Yes, of course, thank you, my son. By the way, are you married yet?"

"Not at all, sir. Not a thought of that... Hmm, hem, there is just no time for that right now. Maybe in the near future..."

"Impossible!!! A VIP like you, the big representative of our dear village in the capital!!! And without a wife to look after you? Impossible!!! Just impossible!!! Let me see... Sola, Sola, where is that stupid girl?"

"Sir, I am in the bathroom, sir..."

"Come here at once!"

The young beauty soon rushed into the room, seemingly wringing the tail-end of her wrapper and smiling nervously at no one in particular. She knelt down before her father.

"Greet Captain here, or you cannot see him?"

"No, sir, please don't bother her. She has already greeted me... How are you, Sola? Are you still in school?"

"Captain," chimed in the chief, "she has finished her modern school now. I was just saying the other day how nice it would be for her to get something better to do, you know, like... like going to the city and doing something tangible with herself..."

When he was leaving for the capital, Captain Oba was accompanied by Sola, his new wife.

He tried from the beginning to consider her as his equal, remembering the opinion of his expatriate Training Officer: "One's wife is a partner and must be treated as such." The problem was, that Sola sometimes behaved rather crudely, and not even her astounding physical charms could erase the consciousness of her inferiority stamped upon Officer Oba's mind. One big consolation remained: She always agreed with his decisions, although she did write home from time to time, to complain about his excessive discipline.

It was mainly to civilize Sola that she was given the opportunity to study as a secretary in Britain under the auspices of the national government. After several months in London, she returned home with a certificate acknowledging her attendance at school, but not much else.

Officer Oba had to think of something to make people look up to him more than before. Since his arrival in the neighborhood, he had won over everyone with his uniform, as well as his wife's status as a been-to. People not only respected and loved him, they were in awe of his position. Something to enhance his prestige...

His daredevil style on his Suzuki impressed everyone, including his darling Sola. She did not attend her friend's wedding, nor Esther's granny's burial ceremony. Her business trip to London was postponed indefinitely, although her dear husband promised to send her to the village to show off her London manners to those back home. "A journey is a journey is a journey," was Officer Oba's way of explaining the new itinerary.

The acquisition of the Suzuki added another joyful chore to Sola's already joyful day. She now got up half an hour earlier than she used to, so as to clean the new machine. The bicycle used to be cleaned, of course, but by her husband himself. Sola saw nothing special in a bike; every Dick and Harry had one. But a motorbike, that was something else! It made the Obas' place a kind of local museum; people flocked there to watch the great officer take off for work and land back home at night. His wife used to savor those two moments more than any other in her short life. There was her own husband, her great officer, a man of the law, his shoulders straight up, his head held high, dusting the already clean seat of his shining machine, checking every little detail before jumping on it with style. He would start it twice, deliberately, raising hell with the engine, then take off with a wild wave of his left hand, as if he was leaving earth for the moon.

"See you, darliiiiiiiiiiing!" she would sing in ecstasy, although he could not hear her.

In the evening, the great officer's return was announced by the noise of his Suzuki, heard from an unbelievable distance away. The custom-made horn added to the officer's class act, and uniqueness. The horn hummed a tune:

Give way to the king
Give way to the great one

Whoever fails to give way
Will be justifiably trampled to death.

Sola used to be very excited by that great sound. Just like a baby with her new toy, she would play with the horn a soon as her captain had parked the majestic machine. He was inwardly displeased at her childishness, but decided to condone it.

Weeks and months of the new money went by in the capital, and all over the great nation. Signs of instant wealth were flaunted in every possible place. Rare models of cars. New clothes. Endless parties. Color television sets and other imported electrical gadgets in a place with electricity only in theory. And, death.

Color television, that was the latest "craze" in the capital. At the ceremony introducing color television a few months before the windfall, the Honorable Minister of Information had proudly stated that black and white sets could easily pick up the programs in color. People were therefore happy that they would not have to throw away their old sets. However, when the new programs were being beamed to the whole nation, that is, to one out of every thousand families of the wealthy nation, it suddenly dawned upon one and all that black and white refused to be magically transformed into color. The first program was a football match between the Tigers of Modafrica and a professional team from Brazil. The gaffe almost cost the Honorable Minister his portfolio, and the President had to call out soldiers to quell widespread riots. The happy few who had been given color sets free of charge, on a trial basis, as lottery prizes, in competitions the winners of which were known beforehand, resorted to hiding their precious gadgets in nooks and corners. Watching a color set soon became as clandestine as a love-affair between a national Minister, or VIP, and a prostitute. Nobody had even noticed during the excitement of the multicolored shows, that the whole exercise was a masterpiece of technical incompetence.

Officer Oba never forgot that historic night. He was forced to leave his dear Sola at home and travel about ten miles across town, to see the football match. It was at the flat of a friend who had brought his set back from America. All night long, they could see only anonymous legs and feet kicking a ball across the screen. When the game was over, Mr. President of the great nation gave a short speech, a great harangue on nationalism and patriotism, and international relations, according to the following day's newspapers; for, as far as the television audience was concerned, it was all a throw-back to the era of silent movies, and more. They fed upon the multi-colored face of the father of the nation, while practicing their capacity to read his fat lips. But it was not a bad experience; not in the least. It was nice to see a black face turned into a many-colored robot. "White man's magic," the great captain Oba aptly called the spectacle. Then, before anyone could really settle down to enjoy the miracle, the powers that be suddenly cut off electricity. This was just as well, because the nation needed people to work hard, not to sit indolently watching television!

Officer Oba himself had given serious thought to purchasing a color television set, but the danger involved had prevented him from doing so. Besides, the importance of such a piece of property was particularly due to its social impact, and his Suzuki definitely stood him in better stead than a box of color kept in a dark corner. Not to totally disappoint his dear wife, who had not yet had the good fortune of seeing natural colors instantly re-created on a screen, he kept promising to buy a set soon. Soon was, of course, equivalent to never.

Officer Oba had one unique habit that his lovely wife incessantly begged him to change: He loved to leave his motor running everywhere he went. He did not mind burning up his petrol, as long as he and others could hear that happy sound buzzing in their ears.

"Darling, you must be careful with that thing, o. Petrol is becoming expensive, and..."

"Don't be stingy, Sola, because I am not," he would chide her. "What is ordinary petrol, anyway?"

"That is not what I mean, really. Somebody might..."

One afternoon, Officer Oba went out on one of his relaxation rides. He had been sleeping all morning, because he was off-duty. Sola had started her usual advice and he had taken off without listening to her exhibition of stinginess.

He rode to Eleganza, a high-society men's wear store from where he had bought a couple of shirts, but which he mostly visited for window-shopping. A large crowd was doing what he, too, was most often compelled to do. He stopped his machine with a little bit of extra confidence and pride. He left the motor running. Naturally.

"Thief! Thief! Ole! Ole! Catch him, catch him, o!!! He is stealing my precious machine. Oooleeeeee..."

A burly loiterer with unkempt hair had jumped on the captain's pride and bolted off. There was confusion. Endowed with innate curiosity, people were converging on the surrounding streets from shops, offices, and other commercial centers. Of course, any occurrence in the great capital quickly attracted large crowds.

"Eeh, eh! You no see dat wild man drife off de beauty machine?"

"Yes, dis wol na wa o! And dem say de pooh caftain jus buy am bran bran new."

"*Ewo!* Tifs don plenty for dis contree now, dem fit tif man sef."

"I tink say dat rogue na magic man, he no even get to stat de ingine befoh im take off."

"Na so I see am o. I belief say he really order de caftain off de bike. Im get gun foh hand sef..."

Thus went the very interesting discussions. Those who were not present during the incident had their own versions to tell the stranger standing next to them. Those capital dwellers were certainly among the most imaginative people in the whole wide world. A sure sign of civilization, one might say.

Officer Oba started a graceless sprint after the man who had dared to touch his windfall reward. His Olympian efforts, coupled with the constant bellowing from his wide mouth, made some bystanders laugh so hard that tears were streaming down their cheeks. Some individuals were running behind him, more out of curiosity than the desire to help.

In front of the Eveready Appliance Company Limited, situated about three blocks away, another crowd had quickly gathered. They were standing in an irregular circle and Officer Oba, still panting from his courageous run, was fighting his way among them. He stopped short when he saw his beloved machine flat on the ground, like a wounded, fallen hero. The engine was buzzing. He paid no attention to anything, or anyone else. Nothing, nobody interested him at that most important moment of his life. He ran headlong past the sighing figures lying besides the machine and knelt down to caress his poor bike.

"Thank God, thank God," he repeated, almost in tears. His wailing crossed those of the two figures on the ground.

There was the burly fellow with hair on him at every spot imaginable. Blood was gushing out of his mouth and ears. His left foot appeared broken in several places. His eyes were wide open, and he was staring at the machine being caressed by his assailant. One very reasonable sympathizer ran up, muscled his way through the curious throng, and gave the injured thief a football-style kick on the head, while simultaneously covering him with all sorts of verbal profanities. The crowd zealously applauded the attacking footballer. Another enthusiastic law-and-order man spat on the robber's face, forcing him to momentarily shut his swollen eyes. He reopened them to resume that stare. Shouts were coming from all sides. Some people were relating strange episodes of the man's mother's unsavory past, others were zeroing in on his personal history as a criminal, while others were busy projecting his life in hell. Everyone claimed to have known him from childhood.

Officer Oba, the angel in that earthly confrontation between heaven and hell, was still blind and deaf to the drama unfolding around him. He had eyes only for his poor machine.

The other figure stretched out on the ground was a decrepit man clad in a whitish suit. His tie stuck out from his neck and his helmet was a few feet away, crushed on one side. The man, completely immobile, his eyes shut tight and a faint smile fixed on his face, was clutching the remains of a television set to his side. Even in that horizontal position, he appeared to be very much afraid that the set might tumble down and break to pieces. Blood was streaming from his skull, and flies were having a field day attacking the open cavity with vengeance.

Someone mentioned calling an ambulance and another, apparently commenting on that suggestion, reminded one and all that the only telephone nearby was out of order. In the meantime, the confusion at the scene became more unfathomable. Insults were mixed with prayers, groans with laughter, and death with life.

Officer Oba, at long last, found enough room to maneuver his precious machine onto the free road. He zoomed off without looking back. Two policemen arrived on their own motorcycles. Their indifferent attitude gave way to a natural harshness and aggressiveness as soon as they had learnt that the victim of the abortive theft was a colleague in the force. They took their turn in pummeling the thief, and one or two blows grazed the body of the corpse hugging the television set.

"Get their particulars, Joe, quickly! These idiots, they never understand that larceny and other crimes won't be permitted in our great nation."

"Henry, this old man is a civil servant, you know. See his pass for the ministry. He works at the Secretariat."

Doctor

My sister, bless her sweet soul, is one of those hard workers that Society only dreams of, but most often never manages to see in real life. Committed, considerate, and conscientious, absolutely. No wonder when she was due to retire from her post at the helm of affairs in a Lagosian institution, the whole community came to wish her well.

She invited me to the occasion, naturally. I half objected, naturally; for, I dreaded disgracing my sister amidst the milling masses of material-minded well-wishers. Linen, as you know, hardly sits easy with lace. A silk-tie never goes with a T-shirt. Clothes, they say, make the man, and a man with no money to follow fashion is but a miserly, miserable monster.

My sister, bless her sweet soul, insisted on my being present, and I had to promise to be there. When I arrived at the church-hall in my Sunday-best safari suit on that Saturday afternoon, I saw elation spread over her pretty face. The ceremony had already started -I forgot to say that, as an African habit, I don't wear a watch- when I sauntered in, clad in my Sunday suit. My sister welcomed me warmly and quickly went to whisper a few words in the ears of the Master of Ceremonies.

"Ladies and gentlemen, I now call to the high table, Doctor..., the celebrant's celebrated sibling."

I thought the MC had called out someone else's name. I was too busy zigzagging through the mass of big-bodied, bulging-buttock lace and silk, to listen to his voice. I settled cozily into a seat, and smiled at my female neighbor who responded with a scowl. Then I heard my name again, and again, and again, with so many eyes simultaneously staring at me, and a few fingers aimed my way like guns at a cornered gangster. I stood up hesitantly, stumbled down to the high table located at what appeared to be a lower level than my original place. The High Table was occupied mostly by VIPs, that is, politicians, people that matter in society. The Masters. The other Master, certainly of Ceremonies, showed me to my seat, the last on the table, and finished his speech.

"And so, ladies and gents, our High Table is now fully occupied by personalities, including, as you can now see, our honorable Doctor, our young Doctor, our own Doctor, here to save us in case of any unforeseen sickness. Our honorable Chairman will now make his honorable speech."

The Chair, in all his honor, with his bulging belly, chubby cheeks, and the smell of new money from the mint, spread his massive frame over the Table and made his honorable speech. The honorable words flowed smoothly, flavored with sporadic saliva, interrupted at odd points by seemingly endless applause, the loudest coming when the Chair made allusion to his privileged position "close to *de Doc* here to save me just in case I should fall sick."

My erstwhile neighbor, all painted and with eyes prancing all over the place full of eligible preys, smiled at me and nodded. Surprise, surprise: so, no more scowl! I smiled back at her and nodded. The Chair's honorable speech continued still, endlessly, *finally* starting from scratch, *finally* repeating statements already made several times, *the final point* returning to already stated and forgotten declarations, while *one single final point, please,* was doubled, and multiplied into several points, until, at long last, Mr. Chair thanked everybody for coming to honor the Doctor's sister for serving Society selflessly with all her heart and soul.

My sister, bless her sweet heart and soul, smiled at me and nodded. I smiled at my erstwhile neighbor and nodded, the destination of my subtle action hidden by the photo-grey lenses of my goggles. Next to speechify the crowd was my sister herself. She spoke clearly, concisely, and made an only final point of expressing her joy and gratitude at the presence of her only brother, the Doctor. Again, the smile and the nod crossed mine meant for my erstwhile neighbor on the low table placed on higher ground than the high one.

My sister, bless her sweet smile and soul, then called upon me, her dear brother, the Doctor, to make a speech. My speech was shorter than hers, naturally, and of course much shorter than the honorable sermon of the honorable Chair. You have to defer to age, and class, so says Tradition. That is why she is taller than I am; why she was being honored on that great occasion, while the only honor I had before then was when I was a newly born baby. My sister, bless her sweet, honorable soul, later told me, when I could distinguish my mouth from my nose, that our father had said it loud and clear, that I would become a doctor. But you must defer to age, and class, so says Tradition; hence, I was a doctor and my sister, bless her sweet, doctored soul, had earlier become a directress. Remember, the longer the word, the greater its importance, so says Tradition!

My speech. I stood, spread my skinny frame over the edge of the Table, smiled and nodded at my erstwhile neighbor, and intoned with all the importance in the world:

"Thank you, thank you very much one and all."

The ovation was deafening. The air was rent by shouts of *Doctor, Doooocccctorrr.* Youth must defer to age, so says Tradition and, from my observation, the others on the Table, even when their age was shorter than mine, had aged longer. The Master of the Table himself, not to mention the one of Ceremonies, seemed a sexagenarian. Hence his speeches (the plural is in order, because every sentence of his constituted a speech) were long and winding. Like my erstwhile neighbor's legs. She smiled and nodded again and, as sly as a snake, I smiled and nodded in return.

Just as we were all about to leave, or to be released, the Chair himself stood and came to my seat. He wanted to introduce himself to me personally. An engineer by training, he had dabbled into business and law studies, then enrolled for a fortnight in a correspondence school of architecture, before settling down into the patriotic life of a politician in our highly respected and respectable nation. I realized that his honorable Arc-Biz-Eng-Law-Pat-Pol, All-Titles-And-No-Talent-But-Chairman, wanted me to recognize his immense talent and versatility. I stood up all the same, and seized his hand in a warm handshake.

Suddenly, he began to sink, ever so slowly, to the floor.

"Doctor, doctor, I'm dying, please, please save me, save me, please..."

What! A doctor without a stethoscope. A medical man with no knowledge of medicine. A doctor of letters with pen and paper for a practice. This had to be insane! People were crowded round me, seeking solace for the sick man, assured that an expert was there to save him. But I was too busy getting sick in my own peculiar way, that is, deep down in my soul. I, the doctor, the lucky doctor, incapable of diagnosing the Chair's ailment, knew my own ailment and the perfect prescription for it. The man was there, down on the floor, gasping for breath. The crowd was still scared, and expectant, looking up to the savior.

I sought out the salubrious smile of my erstwhile neighbor, I mean the one I came to give the appropriate name, *Sane*.

"Silk and nothing else," said she, while shaking you know what, when we finally got together, away from the foolish crowd.

Tiger

Ebene cherished Tiger, his faithful dog. Tiger was snow-white, except for his black tail. He was reputedly one hundred years old, and Ebene never stopped bragging about that to his neighbors in Union City, U.S. of A. Those who had the guts to doubt the dog's Methuselah attributes quickly changed their minds once they got to know him better.

Tiger would read his master's mind; he could think like a man, and he used to wag his tail and swagger around the ladies. His whimpering was read by some of them as a sign of flirtation and many were those among the fair sex who seized every opportunity to caress the charming animal. Indeed, it was generally believed that certain ladies had him do interesting things to them, clandestinely. Any doubting Thomases were silenced by the endless invitations for canine company received by Tiger's owner. Needless to say, all of them were from beautiful, blond damsels. Ebene counted himself fortunate to live in that middle-class neighborhood where the love of animals was as necessary as Christian habits. He was the only African, the only black face for miles around. Clean streets. Pretty gardens. Exquisite buildings. No one seemed to care much for his presence, though. On the contrary, Tiger was the center of attraction.

"Gee, is he ever cute!"

"You can say that again! I wonder what it would take to snatch him away from that boy."

"Hmm, sly, primitive dog, that Ebola boy! I really can't understand how he can keep a dog as beautiful as Tiger."

"Why not? After all, he's been up here for more than ten years from what I hear and, according to him, he's not ever going back to that savage land of his."

"Well, well, I'll agree with you on that point. His home is savage, to tell the truth. But what about all those stories of starvation and malnutrition? The guy's making such a fortune here that you would think he'll spend less overfeeding Tiger and riding big cars, and do something for his starving brothers in his country. What do you think?"

"I think you are just out and out jealous, old girl. Envy won't do you any good. I'm sure neither one of us will own Tiger as long as that boy is alive. I do envy him, too, that half-civilized savage, but at least I'm not blinded by it. Let him keep the cute thing in as much as he doesn't mind him visiting *me* on Sundays."

Sunday was a day of loneliness for many of the inhabitants of Union City. The quiet of the houses. The emptiness of the streets. The hypocrisy of the congregation crowded into the cathedral. The barred doors of the stores. The legislation against any ungodly activities on God's special day. Man must be human, and greedy. Man must be mature and material-minded. Man cannot help following his natural instincts; because that is why he is a man. A privileged biped molding nature in his own image, seeking to better his lot here below, endeavoring to acquire more wealth and wisdom. And you cannot blame him for all that. Only, on Sundays, he has to take a break from his nefarious activities, and act like a saint.

Love is immaterial, and the Union City preacher had, from time immemorial, been dwelling upon the need for more love among human beings, particularly on Sundays. "Without love," he used to say in his rolling baritone, "without love, life is not worth living." So, the queens of the city had to have their fill of love, and Tiger -what could anyone do with a cute, old dog?- filled the void left by absent husbands and lovers.

Ebene kept a notebook listing requests for Tiger's companionship. The book had to be changed regularly. It often happened that, unwilling to take their turns, many anxious callers printed their invitation on the sitting-room wall.

EXPECTING TIGER TONIGHT, LIZ.

MARTHA WILL BE WAITING AT EIGHT.

BRING THE CUTE THING AROUND ANY TIME, JUST IN CASE...

CANDY.

Gifts were sent in large numbers, unsolicited helping hands were offered, and strange acts of kindness prevailed.

Ebene paid particular attention to the Sunday requests, because he understood the importance of God's day. The priest in whose house he grew up had told him that the Almighty meted out double punishment to all those who sinned against Him on Sundays.

"You can't refuse love and happiness to beautiful, civilized ladies on Sunday," he used to remind himself. "Tiger is their only consolation. He makes their day, he brings a glow to their sad faces. He fills a void in their lives. Poor Liz, poor Sue, poor Betty..."

Ebene made sure his Sundays were free, so that he could take Tiger on his visits. He would wake up early and wash his cute dog, comb his silky, blond hair, feed him with the best meal available, much better than he himself could ever eat, and make him relax while he himself took a quick shower. No time for breakfast; too many lovelorn beauties were waiting...

The visits were always the same: Ebene strolled sprightly to the door, pulling Tiger on a leash. He rang the door-bell. The door opened almost too gently and the lady of the house, dressed in a multicolored coat, showed her face, timidly, almost frozen with fear. As soon as she saw Tiger, the fear disappeared. She flew into a spontaneous joyful zeal, grabbed the leash from Ebene's hand, threw him a "thank-you-for-bringing-him," and ran back inside, slamming the door on the owner's face. Always patient, always polite, Ebene would ring the bell one more time and, when the hostess came back, he would tell her when to expect him. She hardly heard what he said, because she was not listening. She did not respond to him. The only words coming out of her mouth were addressed to Tiger. As he moved away from the house, Ebene would hear the echo of the one-way dialogue between woman and dog.

"Poor, little darling, has he been treating you nice? Did you have breakfast yet? What did you eat? Oh, my sweet baby, wow, look at your skin, I think you need another wash. Come on, I know he washes you regularly, but you can always do with a repeat. Tiger, my poor Tiger, come on and sit on my laps..."

Ebene did not enter most of the houses. He did not care to either. He was satisfied to take his dog visiting, he was contented to be part of Tiger's joy. A humble Christian could not, should not, ask for more than Providence gave him.

"I wonder what the boy's thinking all the time. He is always got a smile on his face."

"I often wonder myself... He is too ugly to have such a handsome dog."

"You must be kidding. I've never considered him ugly. His dog is as handsome as they come, so..."

"Anyway, you can forget it. I don't know why I started talking of Ebene's looks. It does not interest me at all."

He was on his way to take home Tiger from his last visit for the day. As usual, at the end of each day of immaterial, human kindness, the young man had total satisfaction etched into his ebony features. He was almost breaking into a trot, so anxious was he to see his dog again. However, he dared not run because, at such moments, the priest's advice came rushing into his mind: *Never try to deprive God s children of their fleeting instants of bliss.* The last hostess might need just those final seconds to bring her joy to its highest point. So Ebene, not about to arouse the Almighty's wrath, held himself in check and tried to walk slowly to the house. He even managed to whistle an old song learnt years ago.

Nearer my God to Thee, nearer to Thee...

At last, there he was at the doorstep. He hesitated. Suddenly, disturbing thoughts crossed his mind.

What if he entered the house? Would Miss Liz be mad at him for intruding upon her privacy? What does the inside of the house look like? What is the lady doing with his Tiger?

That must be the devil at work! He had never asked himself such questions before, and he should not start now.

He rang the bell. A heavy silence, seemingly lasting an eternity. Another ring, a little longer this time. Still no answer. A long pause. Other disturbing thoughts crossed his mind.

Is Tiger all right? What is the lady doing to him? What do all those ladies in the neighborhood see in Tiger, anyway? Sure, he is a dog, quite a dog, but he is no human being. Not like me... But these people don't pay me so much attention... No, I must not think like that, it is sacrilegious to think ill of God's children, and we all are His children. These people have been awfully nice to me, allowing me to stay here in peace and comfort, being very friendly to me and my dog, and all that.

He knocked the door hard, thinking that the bell was probably out of order. Still no answer. He gently turned the door-knob, looking over his shoulder as if expecting someone to jump out of nowhere and accuse him of all sorts of bizarre deeds.

The door was not locked. He opened it, still glancing over his shoulder, then turning round and sticking out his neck to look ahead of him. The whole sitting-room was bathed in light. Wall-to-wall rug. Various colors all blended so naturally one would have thought it was paradise. Harmony. Quiet. Heavenly. Paintings on the wall. Captioned tourist material.

African Safari. Barbados, Paradise in the Sun. Come Have a Ball in Hawaii...

Ebene stepped gingerly on the rug, almost afraid that he might stain it with his clean shoes. He was turning round like a top.

"Hi, Miss Liz, hello! Is anybody home? It's me, Ebenezer, I've come to collect Tiger... You know I have to get up early tomorrow to go to work, so I should go to bed early... Are you in there, Miss?"

One, two, three, four,... ten. It was the first sound he heard since he entered the house. The tick-tock of the clock was not very audible.

"Miss Liz, are you there? It's me, Ebene. I have to take Tiger home now. It's rather late... Miss, are you there? Please, answer me, where are you?"

Perhaps she has gone out for a walk. But, she could not have done that; they never do when Tiger is in their place. Or, she has taken Tiger for a walk. No, none of them does that; they prefer to stay inside with him. He could be asleep... She must have fallen asleep by mistake. Yes, that must be it. Let me see...

Ebene tiptoed through an open door into a vast room with a large, round bed. It was the only piece of furniture, apart from the thick, red rug covering the whole floor. More confusing thoughts flashed across his head. He had never seen such a bed before. A revolving bed covered with a white, rumpled sheet. The clock in the adjacent room struck out one sharp sound. Ebene jumped. He almost tripped onto the bed. He quickly regained his balance and went stealthily out of the room.

He passed through another room. He was met head-on by his own image. Cold sweat came streaming down his face. Eyes bulging out of their sockets. Lips trembling as if they had something tragic to utter, but could not, but would not, did not know what. A disheveled black with symmetrical marks on his cheeks. Bags were beginning to form under his eyes, and the cheek-marks were jostling for prominence with the wrinkles. He looked more like fifty than his proclaimed thirty odd years. Thirty years of happiness. Thirty years of serious education.

Thirty years of resolve to make it in the modern world. He had stowed away to the New World without a penny in his pocket, an ambitious boy from an illiterate family of farmers. He did not send out a word about his whereabouts for years, until he had purchased his first car. Only then did he write to family and friends. A picture for everyone: Ebene in a custom-made three-piece suit, standing proudly beside his limousine. The image of success and happiness. B.S. in Engineering, followed by Master's in Business Administration. A lucrative post with a company paying many times what he could have made back home in Africa. Not in his wildest dreams...

He was about to move from the mirror when he saw some other figures in it, behind his own image. The rich, white hair of his German shepherd. Tiger, the big, gentle dog, acquired when Ebene enrolled in college. Tiger, the obedient dog, polite to his master and his master's friends. Tiger, the frolicsome animal, brightening the day of many a lonely soul with his unique canine disposition. There had been many offers to buy him. One old woman was prepared to give Ebene her house in exchange for Tiger. No deal. They could all share in Ebene's joy, but not snatch it away from him.

Tiger was not alone in that white background. Something else, something strangely human was also there. Ebene turned round, slowly... There was the real Tiger, immobile, perched on top of Miss Liz. He appeared to be asleep. Miss Liz was stark naked, her eyes were closed, and a faint smile was fixed on her reddish face.

"Thank God you are safe, Tiger, thank God! Come on now, get up and let's go home. Miss, Miss, Miss! Miss Liz!!!"

No answer, no motion, absolute silence.

The sheriff called it a crime of passion. Others claimed that it was pure savagery, something atavistic, a throwback to the ancestral habits of his dark continent. Some even believed that Ebene was jealous of his dog, that he secretly abhorred all those people who loved Tiger.

"Poor boy, I hope they will go easy on him. He has been so nice for our community."

"If you say so. I would rather say he's been very strange. I never trusted that boy, to tell you the truth. What did he mean moving into this neighborhood in the first place? There were people like him on the other side of town. He should have gone to live with them!"

"Ah, there, you cannot be serious! Remember this is Union City, we've always welcomed strangers. Besides, Ebola's different from our own niggers, you know what I mean... He has always been a serious boy, a good boy, although I agree with you that those things are hard to escape. The old tribal call can't be shaken off completely..."

They got Ebene the best attorney in town. The contributions were astonishing. They sent him to a mental hospital. When he was deemed well enough by specialists with patently doubtful sanity, he was put on a plane back home to his native land.

Gbogbonyeke, or Peace on Earth

There were five of them, rascally adolescents known all over the small town as "the children of Eli". Their home was the parsonage and their father, spiritual, that is, Reverend Oluwa.

Gbenro was a runaway child who had left home at the age of four and never returned to his family in the capital. He was picked up at the motor-park by the reverend's wife.

Gbeke, a former boxer and the eldest of the group, was an orphan. His mother died during his birth and his father left home while she was pregnant, never to be seen again.

Gbola and Gbolu were twin-brothers from a lower middle-class family. Their father, a government employee, had sent them to live with their sister and her lawyer-husband in the small town. The couple's propensity for fighting made the house unlivable for the twins. Their brother-in-law had the habit of keeping law and order with the whip which fell indiscriminately on both sister and brothers. The shame of it made the poor lady move her brothers across the road to the peaceful parsonage.

As for Seye, the silent "boarder", – that was the name given to every occupant of the man of God's abode – no one seemed to know his background. He was generally regarded as the priest's out-of-wedlock son, but there were rumors that Reverend Oluwa was really sterile and that Seye was his wife's son through a former relationship. According to others still, both the reverend gentleman and his spouse were barren and the boy was a mere walk-on in the family. No matter. He was a well-behaved boy and his four mates were always quick to praise him for his exceptional ways. Needless to say, the reverend and his wife were proud of their Seye.

Reverend Oluwa was fond of all the boys, in his own particular way, but his wife's affection was reserved for another important member of the family, Gbogbonyeke. A "European" cock, Gbogbo was extraordinarily big, red all over, majestic in carriage, ravishing in looks. Mama Parsonage had had him for many years, and, whenever she made reference to her "first child", she did not mean the silent Seye, but her

"European" Gbogbo.

"Look at his fluffy feathers. I picked him out of the last chicks hatched by my mother's fine hen before it was brutally killed and eaten one sad Christmas day. You can't believe it, but I cried when they were killing that poor hen. I vowed to raise Gbogbo as my own child. He has been to every place with me and Rev."

Mama Parsonage used to feed Gbogbo herself. He had a beautiful cage to sleep and eat in. Otherwise, he was free as air. However, he himself appeared to curtail his own movement; for, he never ventured from the parsonage yard. He had the best bird-food in the whole town and Mama actually made special visits to the capital to buy his food at the supermarket.

The other children in the family naturally did not have it as good as the pampered Gbogbo. The boys took turns in cooking meals and their stomachs were victimized by burnt stew, half-cooked rice, almost raw yam, among other delicacies. Mama's tendency to forget to give them money for necessary ingredients did not help any. Their constant misdemeanors, punished by enforced fasting, also added to the growl of their empty, rotten bellies. But none of them dared complain of malnutrition or starvation. God worked in mysterious ways. The twins often paid nocturnal visits to their sister who gladly stuffed them with good home cooking. Gbenro would tag along once in a while. Gbeke had a master-key to the family store. Seye felt it was an unforgivable sin to eat more than they were officially given by Mama Parsonage. His strong nature fought starvation with a vengeance, and his trustworthiness dictated that he keep his mouth shut.

Apart from their individual ways of bringing their living standard near that of the cherished cock, the boys worked together as a team, carrying out lucrative raids at the evening-market. The market was the town's Mecca, the rendezvous of the most loose-tongued gossips, of clandestine lovers, of the best food sold in the community, and that attracted the best amateur thieves. If you had nothing to do in the evening, five days a week, you usually took a walk to the market. If you did not have an itchy hand, you could use your itchy eyes. Majority of the growing girls at the elementary and secondary schools were to be found helping their mothers sell their wares at the evening-market. Potentially fat backsides were fighting to break out of imprisonment of the tight skirts. Hard nipples were hitting hard at clinging, home-made bras. Seductive eyes, aware of the interest aroused in many a sighing masculine heart, were gleefully surveying the apple-snatchers.

The children of Eli ogled not only the backsides and the pointed nipples, but the material booty that their empty stomachs needed for survival. All five of them were there, eagerly dreaming of the delicacies to be stolen, with the exception of Seye, the saintly one, whom they always had to force to join the group. Once there they spread out and lost themselves in the crowd, trying very shrewdly to find a target.

God's children must not starve.

"Hello, Gbenro, what do you want to buy?"

"Just some gari for Mama Parsonage, but she has sent me to come find out the price first."

"Well, the price hasn't changed for some three months; it's the same."

"By the way, do you have any matches here?"

"Only the ones my mother is selling, and you know I can't give them away. However, I think there are a few sticks somewhere behind the counter.. Wait a minute."

While she was gone, one or two stockfish and sardine-tins disappeared with Gbenro.

"Gbenro, Gbenro, where are you? These children of Eli, they're so unpredictable."

Gbenro returned a few minutes later, after delivering his gain into the bucket being watched over in the dark corner at the market-entrance, by none other than Seye.

God will provide for his own.

At another stall, the twins saw one of their classmates, a pretty girl very much desired by Gbolu. She liked the two of them immensely and could not just make up her mind about her Romeo. So she remained on the fence, flirting with both look-alikes. The panacea for Gbolu's disappointment was her generosity whenever her mother was away from the stall.

"I know that reverend and his wife are not feeding you boys properly. Here, take some candy, gari, rice, pepper and dry fish. You must go before my mother comes back o."

"Eh, Ebun, come and see this rotten banana that you are selling to customers. Your mother must be a cheat."

It was Gbolu calling her attention. She turned away, giving her

77

admirer a chance to take some pocket-money from her mother's little makeshift bank.

Blessed are the generous of heart.

Gbeke returned to Seye and the bucket with difficulty. His body had literally swollen up in about half and hour; all sorts of pilfered "eatables" were stuffed under his shirt and baggy trousers. He also had an egg stuck in his mouth.

Seye carried the bucket home on his head, and the others managed with what could be inadequately called bags. Their return was as unknown to their keepers as their departure.

Their room, normally built for the servants, was in the backyard, at a distance from the main living quarters. Hardly did Mama Parsonage and her husband venture into the servants' quarters. A bell was all it took to call any of the five boys: one ring for Gbenro, two for Gbeke, and so on down the line. The room was like a corridor, with one large window and sleeping-mats carelessly thrown into one corner. The other furniture was sand on the floor, a lot of it. That sand was a home for "jiggers", very powerful lovers of human toes. The room also acted as storage for the food acquired at the market. This was carefully wrapped in bags and boxes and hidden inside a mat. The place had an indescribable perfume. The boys' mates at school often wondered whether the reverend gentleman and his wife made them wash in stockfish before sending them to school.

The heroic forays in the market-place and the individual efforts of the five aside, the other means of providing for their needs was the Sunday-evening service.

Man must not live by bread alone, although he should not, by the needs of nature, refuse bread when he finds it.

The townspeople were fervent Christians on Sunday mornings. The church was very often overflowing with sober faces seeking communion with the Almighty. Piety and sobriety were dried up by the African sun, unfortunately. The result was that fewer people went for evening services. The absentees included the highly reputed choristers. The children of Eli were therefore called to fill the void.

And how they filled it! Their croaking was legendary, as was that of the faithful who managed to sneak away from the gourds of palm-wine to praise the Lord before starting a brand-new week on the farm.

The day is past and over

All thanks oh Lord to Thee.

We pray Thee that offenseless

The hours of dark may be...

The common denominator between the morning and evening wor-
shippers was the fear of hell. As Reverend Oluwa used to emphasize in
his sweet sermons:

"Thou shalt not be stingy to thy God; for, He giveth and He taketh.
The poor today shalt be enriched and the rich shalt be impoverished.
Thy fate is in the hands of thy God. So, worshipeth Him, praiseth Him,
adoreth Him, offereth Him of thy wealth, even if it be a penny. Thou
dost not know when His son shall returneth. Therefore, beeth prepared.
Openeth thy wallet and shareth thy riches with thine Savior."

The collection plates, cavernous and shining bright, were full to
the brim, morning and evening. The evening choristers were luckier
than the morning regulars, mainly because the evening congregation
offered what was known as big money. Paper money. Crisp, sweet-
scented bills. Of course, it was easier to pocket paper money than cop-
per. Visions of hell magnified by palm-wine contributed to Christian
piety, and generosity.

Heaven helps those who help themselves.

All the boys from the reverend's holy home went eagerly about
their church duties, with the exception of Seye who looked too scared
of God's house to do anything that would arouse His wrath.

So life rolled blissfully along at the parsonage. Gbogbonyeke was
still there, hale and hearty, sound in mind and body, the apple of
Mama's eye. Then, news reached the reverend that his family needed
him urgently at the capital. It was so abrupt, so unexpected, that all of
the inhabitants of the peaceful house were worried. Mama pleaded
with the man of God that she stay behind to look after the family in the
parsonage, but he said that he could not go without her. The night
before their departure, shouts were heard coming from their bedroom,
but none of the boys had the temerity to go and see what was happening. One of them offered that the couple were raising their voices in
prayer to Heaven for a safe journey home. His mates did not believe
him. Besides, it did not matter whether they were praying, or killing
each other. Just let them go and leave Gbogbo behind...

On the morning of their departure, Papa and Mama called in their
children. Seye, the saintly one, was put in charge and given money for

79

food and other household items. Nobody doubted the wisdom of that decision. Indeed, it would have been unheard of to think of someone else assuming such a heavy responsibility. Mama ran to her Gbogbo's section of the compound, gently carried him up in her arms and gave him a peck on the beak. Tears were running down her chubby cheeks.

"Rev, do you know this is the very first time in many many years that I'll be going somewhere without Gbogbo? Unbelievable, simply unbearable! Maybe he should come with us, hein. Anyway, Seye will take good care of him, I am sure. Don't forget, he is to eat four times a day, and don't let him out of your sight."

Rev was getting impatient. He went outside and started the car. Mama followed, then ran back to look at her Gbogbo one more time. The church bell rang three times. It was Friday. Probably a good Christian had just died, or was it Good Friday?

Seye called a meeting that night. The decision has been taken before the meeting took place: Gbolu was to watch the main door leading to the parsonage and inform any visitor that the reverend and his wife were away. Nobody was to be allowed beyond that point. If any obstinate person happened to go any further, Gbolu, stationed at the sitting room window overlooking the gate, was to call out to the others while holding off the intruder with some meaningless, time-consuming chat. Gbenro was to make fire and boil water in the family-pot. Gbeke and Seye were in charge of the sacrifice to the god of travels, to ensure that the good reverend and his dear wife -and Gogbo's loving Mama- had a safe drive to the capital, and back to the household saddened by their absence.

Gbogbonyeke crowed that night, for the first time in as long as any of the boys could remember. Seye made sure it was his last.

When Reverend Oluwa and Mama Parsonage returned to the fold a few days later, there was no peace on earth that day.

A Question of Economics

When Boniface arrived in the Black household a year earlier, he had his doubts about their beliefs with regard to race and color. His friends had laughed hysterically when he told them of his intention to take a room there.

"They're the most racist foursome in the whole world!"

"Gee, you sure are going to have a rough time of it."

"You better keep your nigger eyes off their daughters, or else."

He had no choice. He was flat broke. His lease was up for renewal and he could do absolutely nothing about it. He had only a conditional pass in his major at college. He was unable to find a summer job; not even the movers, ever-ready exploiters of poor foreigners, would give him a chance. The Blacks were the only landlords for miles around willing to offer him shelter in exchange for some services: For room and board, he had to clean the four family cars everyday, as well as the six-bedroom house. It was sometimes extremely cold, but he did not complain. "Half a loaf," he often repeated to himself, is far better than none." The meals were left twice a day in the kitchen and, due to the pressure of his studies, he was constrained many times to combine lunch and dinner. His *lunchner* was delicious, even if it was uncovered and cold. There were no flies, no cockroaches, no rats. Boni loved the place as if it were heaven.

In fact, he needed only a couple of weeks to convince himself of his, and his friends', mistake. He should never have doubted the authenticity of his new family's proposition. Mr. and Mrs. Black were a middle-aged, God-fearing couple. He did not see much of them except on Sundays when he accompanied them and their two teenage daughters to mass. Sunday was one day when nobody in the family drove a car; they all walked to wherever they had to go. Everyone except Boniface was well attired for mass. He had only a dark suit given to him by his uncle just before he left the shores of Africa. The suit was as constant as the letter K, always neat, with razor-sharp creases. The shirt was a variable, between blue and white. As for the tie, a wide model, one of the latest in the fashion-conscious community, he had acquired it from his last roommate. His shoes were of the latest vogue, but they had pointed toes and their heels were very narrow. The articles of clothing and the wearer showed signs of wear and tear or, according to some pious souls, signs of close attachment to God's house. Nothing to be shamed of, like the church-mouse that kept a life-long vigil in church, in spite of its poverty.

The Blacks once thought of buying their new son some clothing, but piety and humility prevailed. "The poor shall inherit the earth," was the wife's forthright way of encouraging the young man from the jungle.

If Boniface had any negative thought about his condition, it was quickly dissipated by the facts before him. The Blacks never once turned him away from God's abode; they always invited him to the church, and made sure that he accompanied them. They were always together, all five of them: mother and father first, then Suzy and Sandy, resplendent in their gorgeous dresses, with Boniface standing between them. He stayed half a step behind, to avoid knocking them off stride. Besides, by maintaining that position, he could easily see the two girls' back and part of their front.

Suzy and Sandy were no twins, even though most people in the neighborhood believed that they were. They were starting their final year in the high-school when Boniface came to integrate the happy family. The African aroused the girls' curiosity, but they were too shy to ask him questions. Glances were regularly exchanged, politeness was reciprocated, and human consideration was mutually exhibited.

He liked the two girls, one no more than the other. He considered them as his sisters and was quick to defend them against any foul remarks made by anyone at college, or in the neighborhood. The remarks came as a result of the many visitors passing through the Black household. Boniface, confined to the freedom of his basement, hardly saw any of them, but extra footsteps hitting the floor above his head made him think that there must be quite a few people coming by. After dark, seven days a week, the door opened and closed. Feet moved about in cadence. Muffled laughter filled the happy home and, before all the souls retired to savor the well-deserved calm of the night, the original members of the Black family gathered in the sitting-room. Boniface did not for once wonder about the significance of that final gathering. No one asked him to attend, nor did he invite himself.

Recently, however, the night vigil was becoming rather noisy. Voices were raised louder than before and he began to wonder whether there was an argument between his respectable and respectful relatives. His nights became restless and he often felt the urge to put the question to Mr. Black. Mr. Black! *No, never, how could he face him with such a disgraceful question? He'd do better to mention it to mother. He would do exactly that, walk up to her when the head of the family was out and ask her very politely: "Is anything the matter upstairs, ma'am? I seem to be hearing a lot of noise these days."*

He did not ask the question.

"Boni, come up here for a minute, will you?"

It was Sandy.

"I'll be there in a sec."

He had had a rough day at college and was getting ready to hit the sack when the sudden invitation hit his ears. He slipped out of the African robe that served him as pajamas, put on his pants, threw on one of his old shirts, and scampered upstairs.

Sandy, her housecoat wrapped round her shapely figure, was waiting at the top of the stairs. She was holding out a jar to him.

"Could you open this for me, please? It's always getting stuck on me."

He took the peanut-butter jar and easily opened it.

"There." He handed it back to the girl who was smiling mysteriously.

"Thanks a lot, Boni. Wow! You make it look so easy. You don't have to go right away. How come you never spend time up here, anyway? You think we bite, or something?"

A strange question, after all those months of harmonious existence and extraordinary familial interaction.

"Oh, no! Fact is, I just don't have too much time on my hands. However, I see you all a great deal on Sunday, don't I?"

"Ah, there's your alibi! Sunday. Hasn't anyone ever told you that Sunday's something else altogether? I mean, real living together, enjoying life, you know, getting to know each other. Come on, you know what I mean." She feigned anger, squeezed her teeth, and hit her right hand against the wall.

Boniface was feeling rather strange. He wondered whether the others were home. Before he could put his thoughts into words, Sandy told him to relax, that her parents and sister were out visiting a relative afflicted with terminal cancer. The invited housemate became more relaxed.

"Uncle Dave's such a nice guy, you would have thought he'd be the healthiest guy in the world. Poor uncle! He has no kids of his own, but if you saw the way he pampers Suzy and me, you'd think we were his children. He's traveled all over, been married thrice. His first wife died of cancer. The second left him and the third, well, I really don't know how to say this, she took to the streets. She loves too much fun, you know."

In a matter of minutes, Boniface had come to know Uncle Dave like an open book. Once assured that the other relatives were out of sight, the fifth member of the Black family had no difficulty in putting them out of his mind. He allowed a few unbrotherly thoughts to pass through his mind. He seized the occasion to study and analyze his sister's anatomy, all the contours, ups and downs, hills and valleys. He calmly took in every little detail. He liked what he saw and saw what he liked. The taste of the pudding was in the eating. He tasted, and ate, to his, and her satisfaction.

Ecstasy.

The household retained its usual blissful nature, marked by uprightness, decorum, love, with the exception of the two souls that had tasted and eaten, and enjoyed, the sweet pudding. They became inextricably linked by their clandestine act. For one week, the white female felt dirty and sinful. Her sins were washed away after her Sunday confession to God's representative on earth. Yet, she cultivated sweet memories of the singular occasion. The black man's thoughts were clearly marked by a feeling of achievement.

Forbidden fruits are most delicious.

Secret glances exchanged between two beings, unsure of themselves and others.

Keep our secrets secret.

A third pair of eyes must not see.

An unwelcome pair of ears must not hear.

The ecstasy of a few minutes could become the disaster of an eternity.

Sandy became pregnant.

"Eh, young woman, you seem so tired these days, what's the matter?"

"Yeah, what the hell's the matter with you? You keep sleeping all over the place. Maybe you should see the doctor."

"Mom, I just don't feel up to anything. I'm so tired."

"Come on, Sandy, we have to study for that math exam, and remember your average's not real good right now. The guy says you'll have to make a ninety on this test to stand a chance."

"I still feel you should see the doc. I will book an appointment for you tomorrow."

"No! Not a chance, I hate those stupid doctors. That one is no good, and you know it. He'll always come up with some weird stuff."

"Like you being pregnant, ah, ah, ah."

Pin-drop silence followed. No! It couldn't be true, it could not happen to Sandy. Moreover, if it was true, which one of the many visitors would be held responsible? Which one did it? That was not even part of the agreement. Once the fee was paid, the doctor and patient were quits. Nothing more was taken, nothing given. All those pills were failsafe. Only a fool would ever think of the failure of a product belonging to the most modern, the most technologically advanced society in the world. Sandy saw no one outside the house, that was for sure. She and her sister were such sweet little things.

Sandy's figure was losing its shape ever so gradually. Mothers know best, and before anyone else.

"You've got to tell me now! Have you been seeing someone without our knowledge?"

"No, mother! But I did see somebody once and you may not believe it."

"Once? In this house, or elsewhere?"

"In this very house! Right here in this house, mother!"

"But you should have known better than to welcome visitors while we were out. So, you forgot to do what you should have done, huh?"

"Not that, mom, I mean..."

"Oh, my God! Not Boni! Can't be Boni!"

"Well, yeah, mom, I meant, I mean to tell you since. I mean..."

"How shall I tell your father? Poor Harry, this will kill him!"

"Mom, I don't see any problem. I mean..."

"You don't see any problem! Oh, God, what are we going to do? What shall we do?!!!"

"Listen to me, mom, please, listen to me just once!!! I've found out something very important since this all happened: I think the guy loves me, although I still can't get to reconcile myself to that fact. I could be in love with him, too. I've been with a few guys already and, of all the idiots coming in and going out, he is the only person for whom I've felt something genuine. He made me love him, he loved me, really did, in the right sense of the word, the right way, and you can't find that every-day. No matter what I do, I cannot, I can never forget that night..."

"Oh, my dear Sandy, poor child. I never thought this would happen to you, my own child, never! Well, we'll have to see the doctor at once. This can't wait any longer. Thank God we've been able to set something aside for emergencies. I still don't think we should tell your daddy, though; it will simply kill him."

"Mom, I'm not going to see any doctor. Believe me, I want this baby, I can feel it within me. I'm going to have it for me, for Boni, for us!"

"Shut up! Shut up!! You poor little fool. You don't know what you're talking about. Have what baby? And for whom? For whom, I ask, for whom?!!!"

"For me, for Boni"

"You must be out of your mind! Remember we'll be having more guests, the house still has not been paid for, and your car and Suzy's are only half-paid. And think of what will happen when people know."

"People, what do I care about people? With you, everything's a question of economics. I'm awfully sorry for you, mom. You've never been in love and now it's too late."

"So, what do you love? Whom do you love? The fact that a baboon got into you once, just once, is that any cause for rejoicing? Is that what you call love? Does that mean he's better than anyone else? How about those handsome, generous gentlemen that visit us, aren't they worthy of your love?"

"No, mother, not at all, and you know it! You've never said anything about loving those fornicators. Really, we have nothing more to tell each other. I'll tell daddy myself if you won't."

Boniface left the harmonious family a few days after Sandy had broken the news to her father. He had no fixed destination. His exis-tence was in the hands of fate.

Cast your fate to the wind

It might blow you forward
It might blow you backward
Forward or backward
No matter where
No matter how
Just keep moving
Ecstasy. Love. Despair. Hate.
The ecstasy of a passing moment
The disaster of an eternity

Boniface left the Black household a dejected young man, with his feeling of achievement on his mind, a hole in his pocket, and a blank in his future.

Somewhere in the horizon some philanthropic family must be waiting.

Mirage

Like a mirage...
now here now there
human passion disparaged
human vision disillusioned
love equating hate
truth meaning lies
a rabbit in broad daylight!
improbable!
a dog in the mosque!
impossible!
a monkey with a banana!
inconceivable!

Like a mirage...
heart meeting heart
eyes refusing to see
thoughts molding harmony
problems never solved
strangers forging friendship
brothers abhorring each other
races realizing unity
life transforming suddenly into death
virtue is beauty!
hurrah!
Unity is strength!
bravo!
Honesty is the best policy!
encore!

Like a mirage...
Sahara populated
Niger emptied
Kilimanjaro leveled
Victoria harnessed
Blacks harmonized
a full-toothed hen!
you desecrate your heritage
you violate those very rights which
you rave about
and cry about
you denigrate that very race which
you live for
and die for
enslavers and slaves
blacks and whites
whiteys and niggers
civilizers all
and savages too
ball of confusion
like a mirage...

There were several colleges seeking his services, but he chose Booker T. Washington University for an obvious reason: it was Black, *predominantly* Black.

Low salary and unique fringe benefits not to be weighed by the shallow standard of dollars and cents...

A small college with many opportunities for human rapport and interaction...

A Black institution offering the African scholar the occasion to contribute to the uplifting of his race, to the understanding of the plight of his brothers and sisters, an opportunity to fully appreciate, first-hand, all that he had read and digested.

He arrived at Booker T with all the zeal displayed by a parent informed of the birth of a first child. The campus, a small, clean, and beautiful piece of land on the outskirts of the clean city called Harmony, was bustling with life. There were smiling faces all over the brown buildings surrounded by lush green grass. He felt he had made the right decision; he knew he could not be wrong. In his address to the faculty, the President, a very dark-skinned, deep-voiced gentleman, rhapsodized on the qualities of the excellent university. He vaunted the family atmosphere; the unity of the community; the sympathy and empathy; the willingness to give of oneself for the good of the Family; the total dedication of faculty, staff, and students to the Cause; the universalistic approach to Education, Society, and Life, etc., etc. That man had the ability to lift a crowd, as they say. At the end of the uplifting speech, he received a standing ovation. Tears of joy, of appreciation, of devotion to duty, of familial harmony and love, call it what you may, welled in many an academic eye.

The African, though moved by the long talk, could not understand why the hall was being turned into a river of tears. He tried his utmost to show compassion, or joy, or appreciation, or something. Not enough, nothing short of tears was to be appreciated by all those hawkish eyes gaping at him. The consensus of the academic opinion, later expressed to his face by a colleague who claimed to be African, even though he was born in a southern plantation, was that he was emotionally deficient, and that he was too proud and condescending toward his brothers and sisters.

The stigma stuck, naturally.

That did not chill his enthusiasm for the Booker T Family. His contribution, he had decided from the beginning, was to be in the realm of academics. He would teach his students all the intricacies of the French language and culture, and bring them to a point where they would be as frenchified as the greatest offshoots of the Gaulian heritage.

He spent the first day in the classroom arousing the students' interest in learning. The politician and Francophile in him surfaced effortlessly:

"Remember that there are other languages beside English, that the language we are here to study is being spoken by millions and millions of people, including many like you and me. Those sisters and brothers of yours, black people faced with problems similar to yours, are endeavoring at this very second, to learn your own language, English. They would like to communicate with you, to understand you, to appreciate your way of life, to come closer to you, because they realize that it is only by working together that black people the world over can solve their problems. And, as you well know, without communication, Man cannot achieve any of his objectives on earth."

A pause followed by a whisper. A wild-looking, strapping, young man, visibly disturbed by all the brotherhood talk, blurted out:

"Ain't no brother of mine living in dem jungle!"

Scattered laughter among his mates. An embarrassed look on a few faces. Confusion, almost hidden, on the face of the speechifier. He took a deep breath and continued:

"Now, one thing we all must be resolute about is, that we are capable of doing anything, no matter what. Your country is one of achievers and, although people of your race, my race, have long been put down as chronic non-achievers, the facts are there for all to see. A black man, Daniel Hale Williams, performed the first successful heart surgery. The first man to set foot on the North Pole was a Black, Mathew Henson. Another Black, Charles Drew, was the founder of blood plasma. Yet another, Benjamin Bannekar, designed your nation's capital and made the first working clock. So, you see, you, too, belong to a race of achievers. You've got to set out right now with thoughts of success on your mind. French is not difficult; indeed, if you can speak English, a more difficult language, there is no reason why you cannot learn a simpler language such as French!"

The glorious speech was never completed. All of a sudden, pandemonium set in. A couple of students were shouting about fire in the room; another was grappling with a female colleague, while others were whispering, rather loudly, some unprintable obscenities about the instructor's English accent, and the French language itself.

The cause of the chaos was an electric malfunction in the room. The place was filled with smoke and was immediately evacuated. End of class.

Subsequent classes were less eventful, but the general rule concerning attitudinal comportment was already fixed: No one had any particular use for French, or for the instructor.

Mr. Africa -members of the Booker T Family, fixated upon titles, preferred to call him Mister, tagged onto the word, *Africa*, to avoid pronouncing his *funny name*- became discouraged. His state of mind was not helped by the lack of knowledge exhibited by his students concerning realities beyond their own experiences. An exceptionally harrowing event would stick to his mind long after leaving the grounds of the institution: discussion of the first essay that the class wrote for him. It was a take-home assignment, and he had given the students a week to submit two pages on any topic of their choice.

Given the situation in their country, and in the world at large, he never imagined that there would be a dearth of interesting themes. However, he was wrong. Majority of the students wrote about their families, life in their various cities or communities, or why they had chosen to attend Booker T. One of them simply wrote on her paper: "This ain't got nothing to do with French!!!"

Writing material no better than toilet-paper.

A chicken scribbling on sand with its feet.

Concerted effort to murder the English language.

Incoherent thoughts by incompetent minds.

Mutual self-hate among solitary souls trying to survive.

He decided to choose other subjects for them, and to discuss them in class, first in English, and then in the other language.

"Say, brother, we don't know any of dem politics stuff."

He pretended not to have heard the booming voice. Feminism. Racism. Nuclear power. Man on the moon. Rich and poor nations in conflict. War in Vietnam. The Middle East crisis. Travels in other lands. The boat people. Haitian refugees. *Politics stuff!*

"Give us a break, man! Like I figure it, there ain't no way I can go any place else but home. As for racism, feminism, and all dem things, forget it! All we be trying to do here is exist, is all."

He gave up the idea of making them write an essay on *all dem stuff.* He himself decided to live. Instead of single-handedly solving the problems of his brothers and sisters -and they were convinced no problem really existed-, he thought of writing a book based upon his experiences and observations in the modern jungle. He began jotting down notes during his noon-time breaks. Pages were filled effortlessly. Disjointed thoughts. Diverse facts. Disparaging remarks.

"Black brotherhood is a farce. These crazy people don't need anybody's help. They are rude, lazy, ignorant, indeed, sometimes surprisingly more so than whites. The latter, I daresay, are even far easier to reach, to convince, to bond with, than my so-called, self-opinionated brothers and sisters. Everyone is obsessed with the idea of individual rights. Rights here, there, and everywhere! Result of this obsession: loss of politeness, lack of gratitude and other notions of

human reciprocity. Held door open the other day for two female stu-
dents who leisurely strolled across without noticing that the door did
not open by some magic, or that the one holding it was not a hotel
doorman. Rights, still more rights... A white man is polite, in spite of
the much documented hypocrisy and duplicity underlying many of
his actions. I shall always wonder..."

His frustration in the classroom was almost matched by the routine of intrigues, back-biting, and animosities among a large number of
the academic staff. Condescension was the commonest behavioral pat-
tern noticeable in every person with whom he came in contact. His
departmental head, Professor Friedman, was no exception. At the out-
set, Friedman found it hard to believe that his newly employed instructor had a doctorate. He regularly addressed him as Mister. However,
what distinguished the antagonistic faculty from the incorrigible students was the fact that the African had his moments of success with the
former. After the first series of memos addressed by Professor
Friedman to *Mr.* O, the latter, in retaliation, sent off a couple of
responses in large envelopes, addressed to *Mr.* Friedman. The honorable professor immediately stopped the habit of mistaking a doctor for
a mister.

"At best, the books tell half-truths. Only first-hand experience
shows that many people in this confused and confusing place behave
towards you according to circumstances. Convenience, one might say,
governs most actions. A white colleagues comment about Blacks:
'They are too sensitive.' Same comment made by a Black about
Africans. Another white to an African: 'You are not like those coloreds
we have here, thank goodness! All they want is welfare, food stamps,
free food, free everything! They never want to use their God-given
energy for anything. All they can do is, dance those crazy watusis.'
Whites hold down most strategic posts in this college, and yet no one
objects. Gratitude is the general reaction, on the contrary. With the
knowledge of whites' hypocrisy and in-bred hatred for them, how
come Blacks keep imitating them?"

Although Booker T was theoretically open to members of all races,
not a single white could be found among the student body. There were
many light-skinned blacks, and they usually went together in a group.
Any real black moving in their circle noticeably fawned upon them, as
if they represented some kind of dream that he would like to realize, or

a heaven toward which he was aspiring.

Among the off-whites was Linda, one of the African's students. A beauty if ever he had seen one, she was smooth-skinned, full-chested, round-faced, and gifted with those features he used to admire in African women. She also was a bad student, which was rather unfortunate. He could have thrown his professional principles to the winds, and tried to start some kind of special relationship with her. But once he realized that she was a dumb-bell, he turned away and reverted to his supposedly strict principles.

For her part, Linda had other thoughts in mind. She had noticed the glow in his eyes from the beginning of classes, and she never forgot it.

"All these boys and girls keep talking of getting over, but they must be joking! Nobody is going to get anything from me, except what they earn. Linda has that look about her, but I better not read anything into it."

And he tried hard not to read anything into it. She spent an eternity dressing whenever she had to go to his class. She changed dresses almost every day, and she was a perennial late-comer. Hips dancing boogie, eye-lashes bristling with pride, bust erect like a soldier at attention, lips slightly twisted in an enticing smile, she would breeze into the classroom in that slow, suspicious gait of hers. The doctor without a surgical knife would stammer for a split second. A few students would smile knowingly, and the conjugation of verbs, such as *aimer,* would continue apace.

Linda often wondered whether she was making the intended impression on Mr. Africa. Upon completion of the final test before the end-of-semester examinations, she mustered enough courage to act more directly than ever before. The moment of getting over was fast approaching, and she could no longer take things for granted.

The first discussion between teacher and student occurred in his dank office. He was busy writing his notes when he heard a soft knock on the door.

"Come right in," he said, without raising his head from the notebook.

"Hello."

Linda's sweet voice jostled him out of his private world of grief. He dropped his pen and offered her a chair on the left side of his desk. She sat down very slowly, revealing a pair of attractive legs. Seated, she remained somewhat stooped, deliberately, maybe, another attempt to draw his big eyes to the contours of her bulging chest. He saw without having to look.

There she sat smiling for a long minute, not saying a word, staring him straight in the eyes. He could not afford to back down from the pitched battle. So, he stared back. His thoughts went back briefly to his comments on the world around him.

These people spend all their time on material. A very civilized way of life. They are more materialistic than the whites who own the material itself. The Establishment knows exactly what they want and gives it to them in abundance. Sleek limousines, outrageous clothes and footwear, expensive articles, mostly purchased on credit. Bleaching cosmetics, blonde and brunette wigs, masks, and all. Why do they fry their hair? The other day, a student, a very dark one, vowed not to marry any woman his own shade of color. Another student, a rather black, bright girl, bitterly related how her grandmother, an old lady whom she will never see again without thinking of killing her, used to pamper her light-skinned sister while throwing her, the black sheep, to the dogs.

"Well, Mr., hmm, Dr., I am sorry I just can't pronounce your name, well, you know why I'm here, don't you?"

"No, you have to tell me. I don't like to guess."

"Well, you know, I be here several times already."

"So?"

"I mean, I gotta get over this semester."

Eyes twinkling with some nebulous emotions. Glances exchanged back and forth in conspiratorial confusion. Mates in complicity and complexity. Potential mates in the garden of Eden. Hitting the nail on the head? Impossible!

"Well, I don't know exactly what you mean."

But doctors without stethoscope are expected to do exactly that, read between the lines. He could not do it, he would not do it.

"You know, I would do anything you ask me to..."

"Anything?"

"Yeah, anything, and I'm for real."

A long silence. Another knock on the door which she had almost pushed shut with her foot. The ambiguity stayed unresolved. She still did not know whether she would get over, or not.

"Graffiti read on toilet wall:

Dr. Black is a punk. I knows, I have fucked him!
Niggers of New York Arise!
All pigs are pigs are piggies.
A slip while I shit.
Sweetback was here.
Shut up your mouth, nigger!
Your mama."

There were only three weeks left in the semester, and Linda was becoming apprehensive. So also were several others, including an effeminate, tall, pretty lad called Spunky. Spunky went to see him after classes one Friday. The carriage of the second aspirant at getting over was hardly different from Linda's, but the doctor of philosophy's reaction was most visibly different. Repulsed by the behavior of the swiveling Spunky, he did not fail to show his absolute unwillingness to help. He stated that he understood the boy's ambiguous overtures, and told him point-blank that he stood a good chance of failing the course.

Linda walked in while Spunky was on his way out.

"Homosexuality is rampant in this institution and in the city. Stopped my car besides three girls who turned out to be men. Is it a matter of choice, or God-given behavior? Is it natural, or acquired? Why are so many black men, fully aware of what they are doing, playing at being women, aspiring to be females, and in broad daylight? And, from observation, it is interesting that many of them have white boy-friends. The love-hate syndrome of slavery and racism? Ramifications of the overall social stratification embedded in the society? A case of modernity, and civilization? A matter of freedom, and self-expression? Blacks here sneer at Africans. Demythification. Black virility. A big joke. A friend's relevant observation: there is a missing link in black psyche. Somewhere along the line, something basic, something human, has been lost. Irreplaceable. I visited a ghetto with a girl who believes that the best of the crop are sent over to America from Africa, which is her own way of explaining the educational drive of African students here in America. Dilapidated shacks. Filthy surroundings. A dog in a manger. A pig in a sty. Remembering the words of the President commenting on his recent visit to Africa: 'Abject poverty stands side by side with immense riches.' Here, abject

97

poverty lives at a distance from immense wealth, but both are parts and parcel of the same society. And, Africa, what exactly has it got to offer? A question for another day.

"So, have you decided to help me?"

"Look, young lady, you've got to tell me exactly what you want. If you don't, I cannot help you."

"Shucks! You mean you really don't understand where I'm coming from? I just can't believe it! You..."

"All right, all right, you said something about getting over and doing anything I want."

"Yeah, and I mean it! You'll see, I'm for real. By the way, I hope that guy who left just now was not trying to lay something on you. You know the way he is..."

She smiled ever so slyly, and moved her right hand from side to side. He smiled in return. She was certain of success there and then.

"So, what are you doing this weekend?"

"Nothing in particular. I was going to get away from here, but I don't feel like flying this weekend. You know, too expensive."

"Ah, ah, you rich professors, you always talking that way. You only jiving, I'm sure. Now, if you ain't doing nothing special and you ain't going away, I could come cook for you, you know, fix you something nice and tasty."

He was shocked by the offer, or apparently so. He agreed, within a long second, and they rode to his place in his second-hand sports car.

The meal was for real, but Linda was not. She recoiled at the slightest touch of his body. She was scared of being stained by him, and ashamed of being in the company of the quintessential savage against whom her teachers and parents had often warned her. Doctor he might be, but civilized he definitely was not. She did not reveal her thinking, but everything was politely implied by the mind of a guilty professional willing and able to take advantage of a circumstantial underling. He misconstrued her politeness for female shyness. By then, he had explained his outward show of affection by the necessity to separate social life from academics. His apartment symbolized the former, of course.

After a protracted clash of strategies, the doctor without medicine won half a victory. Linda let him see and touch God's gifts to her, without however allowing him to reach heaven here on earth. He felt cheated.

"Black women can be beautiful when they wish. Without the cosmetic superficiality imposed upon them by the mainstream society, they are gorgeous, like untainted African queens. But, like their men, they feel superior to Africans, for no other reason than the fact of their position as slaves of plantation owners past and present. They are a bunch of confused, pompous hybrids groping in the darkness of their civilized jungle. And they would use you any time. They also cherish their light skin, natural, or artificial. Heard that many black women are desperately looking for white men to sleep with them and give them mulatto babies, the ultimate solution to the racial problem. Is it advisable to marry one of them? And, Africa, what of Africa and Africans? A question for another day."

For some odd reason, he was falling in love with Linda, although she was definitely not interested in him. She remained nonetheless fully convinced that she would get over with his help. The semester would be ending in a week or so, and other members of the class had noticed the magnetic impact of her mere presence upon their instructor. Laxity prevailed more then ever before. He had never been a disciplinarian but, with his love for Linda almost surfacing, he found it all the more difficult to control his unruly academic sheep.

"Can't hide love. A female student, one of the rare ones to show any serious improvement during the term, came to the office and stated that getting over with bodily favors was a regular practice in the college. Why did she come to mention that to me? And, was it something I did not know? Is this love of mine genuine? Is it right? No question about it: I do have the right to love, like everybody else!"

The exams took place on schedule. Linda failed woefully. He gave her the grade that she deserved.

Uproar broke loose in the Family. The poor girl claimed that he had made passes at her and, due to her refusal to become stained by the unscrupulous and irresponsible instructor, the latter decided to make her pay for it! Spunky co-signed her protest letter to the Academic Office. At the extraordinary faculty session held to discuss the urgent matter, several colleagues spoke very favorably about the poor girl's merit. To one and all, Linda was a bright, beautiful student full of vigor and totally dedicated to her academic pursuits. So, Linda, bright, beautiful, and black, the apple of every discerning eye in the Family, was asked by the college senate to write a make-up test. A panel of three, with hardly any knowledge of the subject in question, was constituted to oversee the exercise.

As for Dr. Odaran, the doctor without a beeper, the instructor from the jungle, he was forced by professional ethics to move on to another place. He would have wished to stay and clear his tarnished name, but his intellectual brothers and sisters warned him that it would be an indiscretion to try and prove his innocence under such abnormal circumstances. To the last person, they were all sympathetic to his cause, but he simply had to go, for the sake of justice, and in the best interest of the Family.

He would have liked to verify everything that he had read in many a book. *Blacks without the eternal grin. Blacks without a profound love for things white and in between, but not black. Hard-working, fair-minded Blacks. Blacks without disdain for Africa and Africans. Genuinely human Blacks capable of distinguishing between truth and lies. Blacks who are really black! And, how about Africa, and Africans? A question for another day.*

The day he left the grounds of magnificent Booker T, he forgot in his office the notes he'd been taking for his proposed book. His replacement, a sophisticated West Indian with about a decade's experience in civilized circles, saw the notes, and read them. He could not quite decide what to do with them. Take the notebook to the Dean? Or to the President? Keep it in his personal files for future reference? Destroy them?

He took out his lighter, took the first sheet of Dr. Odaran's copious jottings, and almost set it on fire. Then, he suddenly decided against such destructive and negative action. You must not burn a black brother's masterpiece. You cannot destroy his dream. The best way to help him fulfill his great objective is, to send the papers to a publisher since the man had not left any forwarding address.

As he was replacing the half-burnt first sheet among the stack of papers, he heard a rather faint knock on the door.

It was Linda.
Black is beautiful!
Bravo!
Like a mirage...

❀   ❀   ❀

100

Begin Again

Dr. Jean-Baptiste O. Godson, Ph.D. Aeronautical Engineering, Summa Cum Laude, University of Fairville, sat composedly in his rocking chair. His thoughts took him back to the day he left Africa to seek the coveted golden fleece.

The shy, young school-leaver stood there like a pole swinging inside the lavishly embroidered robe bought for the occasion by his dear mother. His shining cap, much too large for his head, was constantly threatened by the powerful evening wind, and he had to fight to keep it in place. He felt naked inside the baggy clothes covering him from head to toe. He was also imprisoned by the boisterous well wishers decked out in their Sunday best and there to send him off in grand style. There was singing, dancing and praying. They all hugged him and almost choked him, and he did his utmost to show his appreciation for their loving efforts to tear him to pieces.

The plane was on the tarmac. He was eager to be swallowed by the white man's flying monster. Its engines were soon whirling in anger. Little Jean-Baptiste, suddenly seized by fear, shamelessly shed hot tears. He saw his friends and family through the window, faceless silhouettes glued to the fence across from the runway, anonymous voices shouting out meaningless prayers and wishes, bodiless arms waving wildly in the African dusk. The aircraft taxied slowly, then started to gather speed. It took off majestically, and his land and people disappeared quickly from sight, and almost from his mind.

His eyes were set on the great golden beyond, the superior nation called Civilization of which he had heard so much. He made up his mind to impress his mentors from beginning to end. A beneficiary of one of the few awards made by the Afro-Civilized Institute to his developing nation, he knew that he had something to prove: that he was worthy of the honor.

The journey was full of surprises, pleasant surprises. The only

101

black face on the gigantic plane, little Jean-Baptiste had feared that he would be ill-treated by one and all. He therefore began by being extra-polite to his co-travelers, a blond beauty queen and an unaccompanied boy, as well as the hostesses. He soon found out that he could relax, that everybody was his friend. He had believed that the journey would take an eternity, that the plane would lose total contact with the earth for so many many hours. To his amazement, he saw houses, water and roads below part of the way and sooner than he had expected, a sweet voice announced the approach to his destination. Then, the plane landed. He had imagined that whites ate food very different from what he was used to. The first meal included rice, stew, oranges, and coffee. He was, indeed, sad to leave the floating wonder of the skies.

At the University of Fairville, he was heartily welcomed by his advisor, a middle-aged war veteran who had fought in Japan, Korea and North Africa. A professor emeritus in History, Dr. William T. Greenberg was a respected specialist on Third World affairs. He did everything to make little Jean-Baptiste comfortable, from the first day to the minute he proudly walked up to the podium to receive his doctorate diploma. Guardian angels don't come any better than the good old prof. He was kind and considerate and his humaneness naturally rubbed on his wife, scion of a respectable family of immigrants from England. Prof. and Mrs. Greenberg hosted little Jean Baptiste in their hilltop villa during every summer vacation. They provided him with a series of well-paying sinecures. No rent was demanded. Food and fun flowed like water from Niagara Falls. Mrs. Greenberg proved to be an extremely gener-ous hostess, physically and otherwise.

Little Jean-Baptiste was grateful for everything, and he cultivated a unique love for the society that bore and bred such model souls as the Greenbergs.

Prof. saw to it that the boy's academic ranking stayed high. The boy was diligent and quite intelligent, but in those risky times, one could always use a little help from one's friends. A little courtesy on the student's part and one or two reminders from the advisor to his col-leagues were not out of order.

"Poor boy, his people must be expecting great things of him, and his performance and that of others like him will only enhance the pos-itive factors of our policy towards those underdeveloped countries. As they say, these boys are the ambassadors and the better they represent their country here, the better their chances of success. Little Jean's simply marvelous. He's respectful, never raises his voice, never complains, readily takes orders, works real hard. You really can't ask anything more. A model student and a modest human being."

The model student and modest human being was still an undergraduate when the magic wand of love smote him. The object of his affection, was, however, badly chosen: little Miss Greenberg! Better a son than a son-in-law. To avert the possibility of incest, Mrs. Greenberg went out of her way to bring into the house beautiful, black girls, eligible and ineligible spinsters all, and well-suited to the boy's advances. Unfortunately, little Jean-Baptiste felt compelled to exercise his independence in such matters. He remembered Kadara, the little girl down the street in his home back in Africa. News about her were mostly favorable; any negative reports emanating from his friends were explained away by their own jealousy toward him and the fact that girls would always be girls, anyway. He decided to send for little Kadara.

The difficulty of getting her out of Africa was soon resolved. A matter of policy: The Afro-Civilized Institute's protégés must be fully aided in their quest to attain a settled, responsible life during their sojourn in Civilization. Little Jean-Baptiste's decision to bring a wife from some ten thousand miles away could only be commended by everybody concerned.

Kadara, the parcel-post bride, arrived on a balmy summer evening. Surprise of surprises: The heat in temperate Civilization was worse than the scorching tropical weather of her native Africa. There she was, sweating like a bottle of beer just taken out of the refrigerator, her thick sweater pricking her body and the panty-hose, worn for the first time in her life, glued to her legs. Little Jean-Baptiste had sent them to her with instructions that they were winter-wear, articles to be considered as necessary preparation for her stay overseas. It was therefore logical that she wear them on her way out.

Her man was waiting for her at the airport. She recognized him from among the motley crowd by his half-drawback hairstyle, his trademark from many years ago, when he was a secondary-school phenomenon, and she a brat taking messages to him from his girl-friends.

They approached each other hesitantly. Then, all of a sudden, she started shouting, "Brother! Brother!", rushed toward him and went down on her knees. Ashamed, he awkwardly bent down to pull her up, muttering that she was starting off on the wrong foot. Two strangers, a big white man and an ever-smiling white woman, were with her man. He introduced them as his *parents*. Kadara, introduced to the Greenberg's as Constance, was astonished at her Brother Omoba's newly found heritage, and her own new name, but she dared not ask questions. The Greenbergs drove away in their limousine. Little Jean-Baptiste and his spontaneously baptized spouse approached his own vehicle. The black porter, looking rather military in his uniform – and she was shocked to see so many blacks pushing carts and carrying things at the airport– pushed the luggage trolley after them. He deposited the bags beside the car, received a tip from Jean-Baptiste, whispered a cursory "thanks," and disappeared. Little Constance shouted after him:

"Thank you very much, sir."

"You're welcome," came the reply mechanically.

The terse response did not offend her, but she was pleasantly surprised that a total stranger knew of her arrival.

"Eh, eh, these people are really something, brother. How did he know I was coming? News travels very fast in this country o!"

Little Jean-Baptiste was caught between amusement and amazement. He would have to train the ignorant child, bring her up to par, and stop her from disgracing him among those nice people. From that day on, he drew up in his mind the plan for the education of Mrs. Constance Godson, nee Kadara Mobolaji. He would lecture her about the fine points of civilized behavior, scold her like a child, and nip her dangerous primitiveness in the bud. Mrs. Greenberg would gladly help in the process.

To expedite the project, Constance was employed as Mrs. Greenberg's Domestic Assistant and an Administrative Assistant at Professor Greenberg's department. She worked diligently at both places, resolute as she was to live up to her man's expectations. She learned to clean various items at the house and became an expert coffee maker at prof's office. Mrs. Greenberg was impressed. So also was her husband who appreciated her every effort and attribute. He gave her little gifts and allowed his hands to generously appreciate her protruding buttocks. It was in fact the professor emeritus that advised her to purchase the latest fashion among so-called liberated ladies, the jump-suit with an open back and worn without a bra. An excellent advice, no doubt; for, in her suit, Constance displayed all her curves.

Little Jean-Baptiste, too, was pleased with his devoted wife. It was a privilege to see her become prof's pet secretary, as well as Mrs. Greenberg's model housekeeper. The civilizing mission progressed rather quickly and, sooner than they expected, Constance was transformed into a sophisticated charmer. Professor showered her with more gifts. Her man didn't complain because Mrs. Greenberg was making him happy in her own special way.

After Constance had spent a year in Civilization, the question arose as to her future vocation. She must not become a mere homebody, as Mrs. Greenberg used to put it. The solution: evening courses in a community college. Constance registered in Secretarial Studies. Little Jean-Baptiste left her fate in the hands of the authorities, a set of individuals with the ability to perform miracles on students, even the most unskilled. Constance could not spell, her written language was atrocious, and her ability to learn, zero. These deficiencies were nullified by her positive assets, specifically, her natural charm. Little Jean-Baptiste did not give a thought to her chances, or non-chances, of success. He and Mrs. Greenberg were too preoccupied with furthering their version of human harmony and affection. The longer Constance stayed in school, the better for them both.

She stayed long and achieved little. The consolation was in her man's achievements. The secretarial program was prescribed mainly to keep her busy, so she did not have to run after academic and professional success, until the night after little Jean-Baptiste was officially awarded his doctorate.

"How have you been doing in that school of yours?"

The question came abruptly.

"Not very well, I must confess. But it doesn't matter, as you have told me many times..."

"No, of course not. It doesn't matter at all. Now, how long have you been there, anyway? Three, four years? Let's see... Yeah, four years, and no progress whatsoever."

"But, Omoba, why all this sadness when we should be rejoicing? This is a day of success for us, the greatest in the history of our two families. I don't understand you at all."

"You will, you will very soon, I assure you. By the way, what do you think of a visit home?"

"What! A visit home? I thought we were returning together, as soon as your studies were completed? I shall wait for you whenever you are ready. I don't want to go back by myself. I think it is time we started planning for a baby. We..."

"Come now, don't be ridiculous, Kadara, we can't have kids now, the time is not right. In any case, it would be very nice for you to go and visit the folks back home for a couple of months. I've written your father and mine about your impending arrival. The airlines will let me know about the flight tomorrow. So, you should start making necessary arrangements."

"No, Omoba, no, oh, no! I don't want to leave you here. I can't leave you to undergo the harsh life in this place by yourself. You need me by your side. I need you, too. Please..."

"No!!! The decision is final. You're going home. Now, be a good girl and get your things ready. Since you can't read between the lines, I'll give it to you straight: You're not worthy of me."

"But, but, I have not done anything bad. I have done everything you have asked me to, since I came here. I have been an excellent wife, and I am looking forward to being an excellent mother for your children. We are going to be happy. We have it made now and nothing can stop us."

"But *I* am stopping you! You seem to think that having a Ph.D. for a husband stops you from making something of yourself. You have been squandering money and time in that lousy school, and you're telling me *we* have it made. You think that degrees are given out free, without any hard work? I had to work like crazy to be where I am today."

"Omoba, please, don't be angry with me. I shall do anything you want me to. I shall begin again, go to a better school, get a degree like you, many degrees, B.A., M.A., MD., Ph.D., everything! But, you have to give me time, just a little time, please!"

"What the hell do you mean, time! Give *you* time? You've had all the time in the world, and you did absolutely nothing with it. You think everything is based on looks. Look around you, there are thousands of women with better shape than yours, but what counts is what they have upstairs. Those thousands, millions, are far better than you!"

She broke down and started sobbing. He was not impressed by what he termed her exhibitionism. The apartment walls were sound-proof, and no one outside would here a thing. He calmly walked into the bedroom and banged the door behind him. She followed him, pushed the door open and jumped on his prostrated body. She was imploring, clutching desperately at the last ray of hope. Her hope died with her tears.

Little Jean-Baptiste, the new success story and the toast of Fairville, demanded and snatched what he called his freedom. Women of all shapes and hues were at his beck and call. He needed the new beginning to re-structure his life to suit the demands of the community of *people that matter*. A nonentity was not good enough to be his wife. He wanted a companion, a partner, someone to whom he could relate intellectually, psychologically, and socially. Someone in the mould of Mrs. Greenberg...

Before Constance could begin again in Civilization, she was on the plane back to her native Africa, to begin again her life as a face in the crowd of nameless millions victimized by life, and by *people that matter*...

As for Dr. Jean-Baptiste O. Godson, formerly known as Omoba in his forgotten homeland, Ph.D. Aeronautical Engineering, Summa Cum Laude, University of Fairville, a rare gem, he had ample time to begin again. He stood proudly from his rocking chair, looked out his window, and saw a svelte figure approaching his door. He opened it with the smile of a satisfied slave.

It was Mrs. Greenberg.

Making it in Songhai

"Gbadebo Amao, Gba-de-bo A-maa-ooo!!!"

The name was echoing throughout the spacious ground-floor of the Public Service Commission skyscraper.

"Where is dis foolish man now? Does he not realize dat it is his turn?"

I scuttled out of the washroom, zipping up my pants, fastening my rumpled tie, and opening the door almost simultaneously.

"Yes, please! I am sorry, I went to the washroom."

"What do you mean? Don't you know what time it is? You have no watch? You were told to be here at ten, on de dot. Dat is how you beentos behave, as if you should be spoon-fed with everyting. Anyway, it is not your fault. Come on, go in, dey are waiting."

I tried hard not to get angry. My wife's imploring advice before I left home kept ringing in my ears:

"Please, Gbade, you must try to be cool with those people. You know their mentality and, even though you've been back here for only a short time, you must by now have got used to the system. Patience, that is all you need to cope, just a little patience. Remember, the best way to catch a monkey is to behave like one."

I tried, I really tried, but, somehow, I could not resist throwing in a few words in retaliation. After all, I could not let that idiot get away with his unnecessary pig-headedness.

"Well," I shot out, "do you expect me to mess on my body, or what? Don't you go to the washroom?"

"Now, you are starting to prove tough like dey say you all are. Look at his tie like dat of a cockroach! He went to de toilet! Are you a washerman, or someting? Eh, eh, do you mean you are afraid of an interview? Don't dey say dat you all are geniuses?"

"If you care to know, I am glad to be a genius. The fact is, *you* are a nonentity!!!"

"Just go in, *sa*!!! I shall be waiting when you come out. Den we will see who is who."

He pointed to the door. It was a door of some very strong wood. Oak? Iroko? Or, was it made of steel? Whatever it was, I had to expend a great deal of energy to push it open. Perhaps my lack of strength was due to my quick trip to the washroom...

"Come in, come in, young man."

"Where were you? We have been looking for you all over the place."

"Yes, you do seem a little conceited. Where did you go to school?"

"Don't you see is tie? E went to America, I am cock sure. Dat is ow dey all dress. Very pompous!!! But, let me tell you right now, pomposity will get you nowhere in dis our society."

I had not yet been asked to take a seat. No opportunity to answer any of the panel's questions either. Without giving them a chance to continue to throw words at me at a distance, I approached and sat opposite them. The chair was very comfortable, although it was nothing compared to the royal stools occupied by the members of the august panel.

"Look at him! Who asked you to sit down?"

"Can't you ear, Mr. Man, or what is your name?"

"My name is Gbadebo Amao."

"You are asked a question: Who told you to sit down?"

"But I thought..."

"You don't tink, you do what you are told!"

"Okay, gentlemen, let us start the interview."

I sat back and did my best to relax. My eyes took in the contents of the vast room, and the figures sitting opposite me.

A rather tall man dressed in white, embroidered national attire, a shining cap perched on his head. A heavy pipe protruding from his lips. Eyes bulging out of their sockets, red, as if they had failed to find sleep for an eternity. The committee chairman, no doubt.

Another Very Important Personality dressed in national costume, all blue, embroidered. Did not look tall, but very broad and thick-set. A chain-smoker. Threw his head back in a sort of reflex action. Puffed smoke into the air and watched it form a ring on its way to the ceiling. He probably had not learnt to pronounce the letter *h* and the combination, *th*, in school, granting that he attended one.

Next, the oldest-looking of the lot. Colorless, absolutely. Smiled from time to time. A strange smile. Must have suffered a great deal in his days. Sad face.

Last but not the least, the most aggressive inquisitor. Disturbingly clean in his European suit. Kept snapping at me, staring straight at me most of the time, to read something, to see through me? Did he perhaps see an image of himself in his youth? Wish I could ask him that one question.

"By the way, your papers show that you were trained in the United States of America. Where exactly?"

"I believe my transcripts are inside my file; I submitted them long ago."

"Eh, eh, young man, why don't you ever answer the question put to you?"

"Well, I did my undergraduate work at..."

"You cannot ear? A direct question requires a direct answer."

"Dat's ow dey all are. Who asked dis pompous one to come for interview, anyway?"

"But, actually, he was already employed as a civil servant before he left for overseas. Is that not true, what's your name?"

"Gbadebo Amao. Yes, I was employed as an Assistant Executive Officer after my Higher School Certificate. When I was leaving for the U.S., I was given a leave of absence without pay."

Memories of those glorious days, all five months of them, at the Foreign Office flashed through my mind. A very enthusiastic, optimistic young school-leaver armed with the prestigious HSC, I knew I was made to streak to the top of the ladder, and to stay there permanently. Delusions of grandeur. Overwhelming conviction of Fate's unique smile. I would become a diplomat, crossing the globe at will, stretching my wings throughout the universe, helping to determine the future of my dear Songhai, and the whole wide world!

From the first day at the Foreign Office, however, there were signs that my dream would not become reality. I resolutely refused to give up. Messengers and half-educated employees competing to show their importance. So-called bosses spending their time ogling telephone operators' rump when not actually having them warm their thighs. Typists claiming to have long legs, thus implying that they would work only when they were good and ready. Only fools tried to be competent, or to show any professional ethics and concern.

111

One reason why my zeal was not dampened was the fact that my time was limited there. I was in transit, as it were. After my training abroad, I would return and clean up the place.

What further helped my self-imposed blindness and faith, was the color and smell of money. My salary was out of this world, and only a few of my former school mates controlled such a high pay-packet. Men of class, we were, the AEOs, tomorrow's chief executives!

Come the twenty-fourth day of every month, I used to take my check from the personnel office and walk proudly across the street to the National Bank of Songhai, where all government checks were cashed. There was the same teller with the supposedly reassuring but really suspicious and jealous smile fixed on her ghostly features, repeating the same sentence every month: "One have to be sure, you know." She took the check, already bearing my signature, and passed it onto the important-looking figure sitting behind her. Thus began the relay. The paper went from hand to hand and, after about an hour, it re-emerged in the hands of the stringy teller who then motioned to me to come to the counter.

"One have to be sure, you know."

"Yes, certainly, it is very necessary."

The pungent smell of the new money and the long wait were soon forgotten, what with the sight and feel of the crisp notes and thoughts of what I was going to do with them swelling my oblong head.

The ceremonial rush to Queensway Stores to purchase a stock of imported teenage magazines for my girl-friend. European apples for my little nephew, nieces and cousins. A shirt or two for my brother and myself. Something extraordinary, such as a pair of slippers, for my father. Something for each of my sisters. Something for everybody and nobody at all. Yet, the cash refused to finish!!!

"Don't dey say de boy as been back now for some time?" The rhetorical question was not directed at me, but I replied nonetheless.

"Yes, I returned to the Foreign Office earlier this year, to my old position and at the same salary, with the usual computerized increment."

"Who is asking you to bring in the computer here? What has that got to do with the business we are tackling?"

The last speaker, I confirmed, was having quite a hard time keeping his eyes open. I said nothing more. There was a strange, one-minute silence.

"Well, at last," said the chain-smoker, "I see here that you are a linguist."

"Not really. I specialized in literature, French metropolitan, French-Caribbean, French-Canadian literatures. For the French metropolitan, I took particular interest in the twentieth century, and my genre in all of them is the novel, although I read a lot of drama, and I write some poetry in my spare time. Moreover..."

"You have certainly done a lot. Anyway, of what use is all that in the Service, especially when you have gone and taken an M.A?"

"Eh, eh, so e as a Master? But you look so young. Ow old are you? Don't answer dat, I see it ere. Are you sure you ave an M.A.?"

"You know all these boys; when they go overseas, they are never satisfied with a B.A., which is what we really need in this country of ours. M.A. this, Ph.D that, D.Sc another thing... I don't know what they want to do with all the papers. Over qualification, a major problem that has to be urgently dealt with."

"So, Mr..., what is your name again?"

"Gbadebo Amao."

"Yes, Mr. Amao, you say you are not a linguist? What have you been doing at the Foreign Office?"

It all came back to me in a rush, clogging my head, nauseating, disgraceful, unbearable. I recalled the renewed enthusiasm of the early days of my return, and the fatherly voice of my Head of Division welcoming and encouraging me:

"Good to see you back, young man. I remember you from several years ago; you are still the same confident young man who left us; only, you have lost some of your hair."

We both laughed heartily. We both knew that, before long, I would lose my appetite for the diplomatic life of lies.

The Diary of A Lady Called Desire

Dec. 24 – America, so this is America. I arrived yesterday, my first flight ever. Interesting to be in an aero plane, thousands of feet above the ground, gobbled up by the clouds, with other aircraft floating some distance away, each plane following its own special route in the air, like human beings following their destiny. I was very frightened and I once had to run to the toilet to vomit. The old lady sitting next to me tried to be nice, she was nice. The hostesses, too. Understanding people, these whites. They are capable of many miraculous things, like their planes, skyscrapers, telephone, etc.

Femi met me at Kennedy International Airport. He has not changed much; a little chubby, receding hair-line, a little lighter in complexion, a little colder in disposition. My first Christmas away from home. Hope it will be beautiful and happy. It will be beautiful. Femi is there.

Dec. 25 – The party. So many compatriots singing American jargon better than Americans. All those pretty attires, marvelousY But I felt as if I was back home, all the same. Lace, brocade, jewelry, Heineken's beer, juju music. Femi appeared to be hiding from something, or someone. Only one dance with me, but that was enough, it lasted thirty minutes, a swinging piece full of words of wisdom. That Lady in the corner with eyes like those of an owl, why was she staring at me all night? I shall ask Femi when we're in bed tonight. Oh, I'm so happy, so so happy! America! America!

Dec. 26 – That lady staring at me, she showed up at the apartment again yesterday. Nothing really special about this Christmas. The streets were all empty, the whole atmosphere was strange. And that white stuff on the ground; very beautiful to look at. Turkey, the apartment had turkey-smell all over it. The people will likely give birth to turkey the way everyone was swallowing the heavy stuff. I would give anything to have some chicken.

Femi did not give me a chance to mention the strange lady. He did not sleep at home. I shared the apartment with visitors from out of town. Extraordinary hospitality. Come to think of it, my husband has not slept with me since my arrival. What will happen to the child? He must know, he cannot know! I have to tell him. But how?

Dec. 31 – The past few days have been hell. So lonesome, so alone. I feel like going back home. But I can't, I dare not. The baby, remember the baby. What does Femi do with his time? We have hardly been alone together for up to an hour, he's such a popular fellow, all his friends love him, and he is extremely well-off, too.

The mysterious woman must be living close by. If she comes back tonight for the New Year's Eve party, I'm going to make trouble. I shall show her what an African woman is! Femi's girl-friend? His second wife? Impossible! All the rumors reaching me at home are false, false, false! But who is she, anyway? Is she white or black? Hard to tell which is which. She is so pretty, at least I have to congratulate Femi for his good taste. I must ask the question tonight, I must!

Jan. 1 – I wish I could forget last night, but how can I? So, it is all true; I just can't enter the year with such a heavy load on my mind. All those rumors have been substantiated. Femi, my own Femi, he must have been pushed into it. American trickery: treacherous woman, devilish Eve, she offered him the apple and he was unable to resist. What can I do? I shall return home... But I dare not. The baby, what am I doing here? What shall I do? I have to tell him the whole truth, but he should have a lot to tell me, too. If he does not, I will not. That lady, I must send her name to Mama for quick action. She must pay for her treacherous ways. Femi continues to stay away from me. Tonight, he has to take it, I shall give it to him, force it on him, I still have the old magicY Do I? What am I going to do?

Jan. 2 – Thank God, he finally took it! What a great relief! Strange, but he seemed to have forgotten my name, since he kept calling out softly some name like Debbie. He was reeking alcohol as if his whole body had been dipped in a barrel of a concoction of *ogogoro*. Napoleon brandy, cointreau, Jamaican rum, and vodka. He took it, he took me, and that's all that matters, even if he called me Devil, even if he smelt like sewage uncleared in a million years. He took it, he finally took it. He has made his baby, our baby!

Jan. 5 – God, help me, please! Help me! Femi is refusing his baby, he has decided to send me back home. No! How can I face the music back there? I have hardly completed a month here, what shall I do? If only Mama were here now, I wonder, did she get my letter? I can't write

116

her now, it is getting late. If Femi sends me away, I shall kill myself! That ugly whitish woman, that prostitute, it is all her fault, everything is her fault. She has stolen my husband from me. All these nasty Americans, that is how they are. What shall I do? God, please show me the way, show me the light, please! I'm going out of my mind. Where can Femi be? I have to talk to someone, but who? Where are Femi's friends, where are all those nice people? All the doors here seem eternally shut. God, I'm so alone...

Jan. 7 – Mama's letter... She has not yet received mine. She's sure that everything will work out for the best... the eternal optimist. Wonder what she's doing now, probably praying to God, thanking him for all He has done for her only daughter. And here I am, all alone, in a foreign land, carrying a double burden, uncertain of the outcome. Mama has included a rather long list of things to be sent to her – 'Don't worry if you can't do it now, my Daughter. I can wait until you've settled down,' as if I'm here to make millions... if only Femi would be reasonable with me... Lord, I'm so alone here.

⊕   ⊕   ⊕

On January 13, a neighbor phoned the police to report a strange noise in the Africans' apartment. Six squad cars sped to the scene. They had concern spelt on their faces. Maybe a life was being lost, and something had got to be done at once to save it. Life is so precious. Civilization boasts of its low mortality rate, exceptional technological know-how enhancing its capability to preserve human existence. An ambulance arrived almost at the same second as the police cars. A crowd started to form, a crowd of humane and concerned citizens of the Great Society. Volunteers asking sincerely what they could do. Prayers for the victims' safety. Love for strangers, love of life, love for fellow human beings. Some were shedding hot tears, others were sighing in resignation. A premonition of death, a last ditch effort to preserve, to save life...

Femi's woman, abandoned in the old apartment, had unsuccessfully tried to hang herself. The will to live combated the desire to die, and won. An awkwardly tied noose slipping from a restless neck. The scream from a throat unwilling to forever part with its sounds, even though they were of silence. The police broke open the locked door and found the

117

woman bathed in cold sweat, in a fainting fit. The ambulance rushed her to the hospital where she was revived in no time at all. They checked her papers, as a mere formality, for the records: she had a visitor's visa for two weeks. A good thing she survived; she would have created problems for the great authorities of the Great Society.

She would be put on the next available plane back home to her beloved Africa.

A Pint of Blood

Why are children born?
That they may live long and die old.
Why are children born?
That they may live short and die young.
But why are children born?
That they may jell into precious jewels and bring
joy into the dreary lives of their parents.
But why are children born?
That they may languish and linger and lapse into
a coma and perish in peace.
But tell me why are children born?
That they may live that they may die in life not
lived in death everlasting.

There he was on the hospital bed, a few years old, they said, according to the records kept in the municipal office. Alive or dead, maybe more dead than alive, motionless, whimpering a little bit, his eyes wide open, staring at the wall, or at something no one else would ever see. In a world all his own. All round him there was life. Nurses in starched white frocks with creases sharper than the doctor's scalpel, were shaking their hips like models on a lit stage ogled by the loaded robbers of high society. Their faces bore a fixed smile which expressed the love of life, or of death. Certainly, they were not smiling at any of those bodies tucked into the stinking sheets. Yet it was already something, to smile, even if you were smiling at no one, or nothing.

Wailings in the night. A baby, her body half-burnt, sat on her bed clinging to her grandmother's hand, her life ticking away by the second, her wailing becoming fainter by the minute, and the doctor's lateness becoming longer by the hour. A little brat of about three had his two legs tied dangerously to the bed-posts. He had cried all day long for his mother who had abandoned him on the very day of their accident in a public vehicle bringing them back from the market where she used to sell vegetables. Father had left them both after a petty quarrel over the cost of baby food for which he used to contribute half, irregularly and reluctantly. Mother would come, but the little boy would by then be dead. He did not know, he would never know of her coming. The kind-hearted nurses had a ready story, as usual: Mother went to get him his bicycle and should not be long. The doctor had told them that his legs would be amputated, that the poor thing had infection and other newly detected diseases, and no chance in the world for survival. And the poor thing kept crying, while waiting desperately for Mama.

His neighbor was also a boy, only older by a few months, and wiser. He had been in an accident in which his head was badly smashed. He had lost both parents and his only sister in the ghastly crash. He saw their remains being dragged out from under the overturned bus. He just lay there, mouth agape, not resisting the friendly arms that carried him into the ambulance and on to the hospital. A year had already gone by. Still no word from the wide-open mouth. Still no batting of the staring, startled eyes. Still no life in that dead body. Still no death to that living being.

Other bodies lay in the beds of that lantern-lit room. They were all young but decimated by life. They were all alive but taken hostages by death. Their night was like their day, monotonous, morbid, and mad-dening. If only the awe-inspiring Christ overlooking the ward would wave his wand and make them well. If only the nurses would get mad at them, shout at them, do something human! If only the doctor on call would come on time, or late!

The night dragged on, punctuated by whining and wailing. A cat meowed and scratched, cried like the real baby writhing in pain in the creaky bed. A dog barked at a figure stealthily groping his way in the dark alley. An owl ululated in unison with the drums of an unknown village praising the power of its silent gods. And the young ones cried in their awakened sleep, clinging to the arms of mother who was away in the bed of her hypocritical, lecherous lover. Later, much later, a cock crowed loud and long, almost simultaneously with the church-bell. It was the dawn of another day.

He lay motionless on his bed, three years old, they said. Alive or dead. He was crouched in a semi-circle, a kind of boomerang, an everlasting link between mother and father separated forever. The nurses just passed him by, as if he was not there. They had done their duty towards him, and that was enough. A routine call to the doctor on duty, not on the dead telephone, but through the ambulance driver who took all the time in the world to discharge a duty that afforded him the opportunity to stop over at the bar-restaurant on his way to the doctor's house. He knew that he did not have to hurry; for, the good doctor -was he not supposed to be in his office in the first place?- would not be home. Right he was, as usual. Upon his return from the useless errand, the driver reported the scene to the nursing sister, a rascally grin on his moon face.

He knocked on the door, very politely, afraid to disturb the big man behind the big, locked door. No answer, none until he had mustered the courage and strength to hit the damn door until his hands began to hurt. Then, the door was opened, and a face peeped out, very slowly. The voice was so thin that he feared being confronted by a ghost.

"Yeees, whom do you want, please?"

"Oga dey for house?"

"Come again, please. You want somebody?"

"I say oga dey dere? I mean, docta, him get to come for osipita quick quick. Case dey for grand."

"Huh, he's been away all morning, and he is supposed to be right there at the hospital. Are you sure he is not there?"

"Madam, I sure well well. Na small pickin dem just bring and de case na serious one, o. And, de oga wey get to come las night, im not come sef."

"Well, well, I shall give him your message. Pity I can't help you much. There are a couple of places I could check but, as you can see, I have got my hair in rollers, and I am about to give it a quick run of the hot comb, since I have no time to go to the hairdresser's. So, you people at the hospital will have to be patient. I"m sure JT won't be too long getting there."

"But, madam..."

He could not finish his sentence. The door slammed hard and firmly in his face, and he heard the ghost shouting in a totally different tone inside the house. Her voice was soon lost in a cacophony of odd noises, like things being thrown around, like hell breaking loose in heaven, like the devil being exorcised from a beloved deity. Try as he did, he could not understand the ghost's angelic madness. Nonetheless, he believed he should have understood: Ghosts were different from ordinary human beings. Driving back to the hospital, he stopped once more at the bar to rest his overworked body with a draft of palm-wine and a handful of the kitchen hand's backside. *Man no fit die for anoda man s work, o.*

The sister hardly reacted to the story that made the man grin so enthusiastically. She had heard more interesting tales before. She was only concerned with the mixed odor of palm-wine, inferior, imported rice, and natural bad breath emanating from the big mouth decorated on either side by a thick, white spittle that hung dangerously to the skin and danced to the rhythm of the ever-moving cavity. She had often told him to collect some mouth-wash from the pharmacy. She wondered whether he could smell his own breath and experience the feeling of potential vomiting about which many of their co-workers were regularly complaining. She was about to tell him to shut up, to go brush his teeth, or something, when she recalled that he had sworn on his insane father's sanity that, every morning, he did use mouth-wash collected from the pharmacy. Of course, the mouth-wash was carefully diluted with water, so that a few extra bottles would be available for sale in the good sister's chemist-shop.

And he lay motionless on the dirty bed, alive or dead, three years old, waiting for the good doctor. It was morning, the same morning his mother took him there. She was crying out of love and fear. *Oh, God Almighty, don't let me lose my baby, he is the only joy that I have in this world. If he dies, I will kill myself, and I will come to hate You for snatching him away from me. You must know that I have suffered, you must know how much happiness I have had these past three years...*

She hugged him to her heart as if someone was about to steal him from her. The nurses had to be very persuasive to succeed in taking him and putting him on the bed. *Oh, God, don't let me lose my baby. If I do, what will happen to me?* They took one look at him and realized that he needed the doctor, immediately. Dilated, expressionless eyes. Body long like a beanpole, hot in spots, cold in others. And he had spent three years of endless motion and extraordinary élan. His mother used to fear that he was too active, that he would hurt himself. No sign of any illness, he was never ill, until the night when he, the voracious eater, the envy of all the parents in the neighborhood, the healthy kid, the symbol of life itself, refused to eat, stopped talking, became ill. *Oh, God how can You take my only child!*

She and her husband had been married for ten years before Oluwafemi came. Ten years of hopes built up, lost, and found again. Ten years of heaven turned into hell and back to heaven. He was a messenger when she met him at the company entrance. She hated him at first sight, with his fat head, impish smile, and cynical disposition. She was a typist at the General Manager's office, with an eye for men and money, although not necessarily in that order. She was a beauty, and she knew it. Everyone, especially those who mattered, including the GM himself, used to allude to her charm and comely figure. The only critic who remained unimpressed was that stupid, clean, good-for-nothing messenger. She wished she could spit on his face, slap him, or send him away forever to an island populated by animals. She ended up marrying him.

Ten years of love and harmony, sometimes. Ten years of lies and hate, sometimes. Ten years of hurt and love, all the time. From the very beginning, they wanted a boy, a big, bouncing baby boy. To train and give all the things that they themselves never had in their lives. The messenger started as a gardener in a distant relative's home after having been forced to abandon school because he could not cope. He graduated to the post of messenger through the grace of another distant relation who believed that everybody was God's child and deserved a chance in the shade. As for the typist, she had aspired to become a full-fledged secretary, shorthand, typing, coffee-tray. A private room next door to the boss, minute-pad in hand, telephone, and all. However, she had not reckoned with the necessity to pass a few examinations.

The messenger managed to survive in the jungle of bureaucratic jargon, doctored and shredded papers, and worshipped personalities. He toadied to the high-ups, tended the tender egos of the middle cadres, and teased his empty-headed colleagues into believing that they were the masters' equals. Perfecting the politics of personality-pampering and self-prostitution, he came to enjoy a certain level of respect in the company, and outside. At the same time, the typist, her inability to pass exams notwithstanding, found consolation in her natural charm. She used her body profitably, shared the borrowed beds of a few important slouches, and gained the respect of those who mattered, that is, the morally destitute superiors, as well as the equally despicable inferiors.

Ten years of hurt pride, and pampered hearts. Ten years of money in the bank, and moral bankruptcy. But love conquered all, love helped the heart to forget the pain, love helped you to hold high your drooping head. *If you pimp your soul, if you prostitute your very self, it is because you cannot do otherwise, it is because society would not give you a chance, and you have to live, or die.*

Jimi and Tinu loved each other, and they forgot the dark past during those ten years of waiting for Oluwafemi to come into the world. Only when the waiting became prolonged, too prolonged, did the memories strike hard at the tender cover used by the resisting soul, to hide shame and fear and despair. *I hear all about you, you harlot! And I know all about you, too, you eater of another man's shit! Well, if it is true that a leopard cannot change its spots, it is also true that a man with bad eyes wears corrective lens, and manages to see, even if he is reduced to seeing double, or mirage, sometimes. And you can paint over annoying spots even if you cannot wash them clean, and the new color could cause you new problems. And you can pay a token sum on your debts even if you are unable to totally appease your hound of a creditor who actually stole the money before passing it to you. And love does placate the souls of two sinners who would rather see each other dead than come to the lowly estate of experiencing true love.*

Tinu and Jimi loved each other and they buried the past on the beach, in the bank, and in bed. Tinu was pregnant three times, and three times she lost the baby. The first time did not bother them at all; the second did not bother them much, but the third bothered them so much that they were convinced that it was the work of some evil hand striving to empty Tinu's womb of its most cherished fruit. Since the Christian God had failed in His duty, they decided to see their grand-parents' God, in the person of the local medicine-man. Amulets, cowry-shells, tattoos, palm-oil, a black cat, rank odor, in a round mud-hut in the middle of nowhere. A decrepit, old man surrounded by a paraphernalia of perfumes, pans, pots, panache, and an illegible sign on the wall decorated by a picture of a figure resembling Jesus Christ. They followed Jimi's ex-school-mate-become-businessman into the dark hut. The leader knew his way while they were groping in the dark. He moved confidently to the shrine from where came a funny noise, said a few indecipherable words, and called out to Jimi to hold his wife's hand,

and to approach. Jimi obeyed, with a bit of difficulty since Tinu was trying to find her way back to the door, and out of the darkness.

"My children, God Almighty loves you. He is fully aware of your
problems, and has decided to come to your aid in this your hour of
need. But you must promise to serve Him till the end of time, with your
life, with your material wealth, with all your money, with all your soul."

The word, *money*, made the couple shudder in unison. They had
some, but you can never have enough in our society of greed and graft,
of material deification and moral degradation. Money matters most,
but a child is your only chance to cheat the charity of the rich. They had
no choice but to rush to the bank and empty everything into the waiting hands of the medicine-man. They were back at square one, finan-
cially. Tinu became pregnant soon afterwards. Jimi worked like a dog.
In the office, and outside. The messenger's uniform in the morning
became the taxi-driver's outfit in the afternoon. The dark, furrowed
brow by the day was transformed into the masked, cotton-smooth robber's face by night. Bags of cement developed feet and ran en masse
from the government's ship to the warehouse of a patriotic tycoon.
Cartons of beer emptied themselves from the trucks of the rightful
owners into waiting vehicles heading for unknown destinations. Money-
bills still smelling the odor of the mint disappeared from armored cars,
and landed mysteriously at the home of the innocent Executive
Director of the National Bureau for Banking. Jimi was one of a nameless, faceless crew out to make a living, a pawn in the hands of the privileged few that did not have to lift a finger, messengers of death, and
winners of blood money that was still chicken-feed to the rich.

Tinu, poor woman, was unaware of her man's actions. She asked no
questions, good wife that she was. She was too happy to have food on
the table, and her sweet little one on her back. On the night of
Oluwafemi's sudden sickness, Baba was away on an ostensibly long
journey that took him only to the other side of town, to the house of a
tycoon employer whom he and his stocking-on-the-face friends considered too miserly for their liking. His dead mother was ill in a village
that he had never visited in his whole life, and he would be back late
that same night, or very early the next morning.

It was a routine evening. Mama returned from work around five,
ate, changed her clothes and the baby's, lay on the sofa where he came
jumping on her while logging miles on his many trips to Baba's room,

which was also Mama's room, and the baby's own playroom. She fell asleep, as usual; woke up at the sound of a passing motorcycle which she mistook for Jimi's, as usual; went back to sleep, and finally woke up at the shrill cry of Oluwafemi who had fallen off a chair, as usual. It was becoming dark, and the boy was calling out for Baba. Not unusual. Baba always came home very late these days, long after Mama and Oluwafemi had embarked upon the temporary journey to the land of the dead.

What was unusual was the fact that the little boy kept running to the door, peeping out and crying shrilly, running back into his mother's arms, and repeating the same action over and over again. Tinu was becoming worried, but only a little. The boy was probably tired and should settle down after supper. She prepared his food. He refused to eat. He stopped talking. His body became hot, and then cold, hot again and, finally, cold. The last word he uttered was, *Baba.*

She did not sleep a wink all night. She washed him with cold water. She gave him some of the potion brought by a neighbor who had come visiting and seen the boy shivering. She prayed to God, read her Bible, and lit a candle. *My children, God loves you. He knows all your problems and has decided to come to your aid in this your hour of need. But you must promise to serve Him till the end of time.* But, how can you promise to serve God till the end of time when you have to live here below? How can you promise, when life itself is a broken promise? How can you promise to serve the god of heathens, hidden away in a house of mud, represented by a man in tatters? *Oh, God, don't let me lose my baby, please!* And the candle was burning ever so slowly. The night, as long as a hundred-year jail term, finally reluctantly gave way to morning.

She took the little thing to the hospital. *Why did you not bring him here as soon as this thing started? You must be a fool, you irresponsible woman! And a witch, and an ass, and a prostitute, and the devil himself!* The nursing sister knew a dead child when she saw one. Yet, you don't go making a prognosis of death to a woman who will take death for life if only to keep herself going. But, who knows, the boy may pull through, his mother's faith may help, and the doctor's expert intervention, too.

The doctor on duty was still not there. The good sister had seen too many cases of neglect in her time. She had become used to them, naturally, particularly after the same damn thing had happened to her only son.

Tinu, almost delirious, would not part with the boy. *Come now, you can go to work, he will be fine. He just needs a little rest, that is all. By the time you come back from work, he will be ready to go home, believe me. Let them have him, hein?* So, you let them have your son, your only son. The piercing eyes, the smiling face, the sweet words, flowing slowly out of the mouth like the waters of a peaceful stream. And you let them take your baby boy whom you love to death even when you don't know what it is to love. You let them deceive you even when you know very well that lies are the law of the land.

Tinu was persuaded. She let her baby go. She went to her office where she was a low-status star, or a near nobody.

And he lay motionless on the bed, alive or dying, or dead, all of three years old, waiting for the good doctor. Black flies with heads like electric bulbs, with eyes sticking out of the bulbs like powerful light in pitch darkness, buzzing caterpillars invading long abandoned putrid food, zealously shared the bed with the poor boy. They covered the helpless body, carving out of his brown skeleton patterns of which Picasso, as well as other European icons borrowing but not acknowledging the artistry of Africans, would have no doubt been envious. From time to time, they would break into an incomprehensible song to which the boy seemed to dance with a twitch of his shoulder.

And the nurses passed by, blind to his presence, engaged in their important responsibilities, having performed their duties towards him. Human nonchalance contrasted with insect enthusiasm. Insect sing-song was complemented by human croaking. His lack of motion and apparent peace meshed perfectly with the liveliness of the surroundings.

And still the good doctor did not arrive. And he lay there motionless, all of three years old. It was late morning and many of the co-tenants of the dormitory were asleep. Suddenly, a cry of woe broke the sonorous silence. *Oh, my God, he is dead! He's deeeeeeeeeeeeeeeeeeeead, oooooooo!!! The only reason I am living, the all in all of my presence on this senseless earth. They have killed him, o. I knew they would kill him! The bastards! I never knew it would be so soon, o.* The nurses at once showed the aggressive, desperate woman that she, not them, was the bastard. *How dare you disturb the peace of the sick little ones!*

127

What an irresponsible old hag! Get out of here before the lightning of some sweet, sweaty palm hits you on your dastardly, pimple-riddled face! Oh, my God! Your God, my ass!!! And, don't you see that he is still breathing? Come, come, the doctor will soon come, and he will confirm to you that the dead boy is alive. As usual, lies gave back life to death.

And he lay there dead to the life of lies being played out around him. And you might say that he, all three years of him, was fortunate not to be a party to the human comedy. Yet you would not be taking into account his opinion, the opinion of an innocent three-year-old with the energy to live till a hundred, a three-year-old now lying there, waiting for the good doctor.

And, then, the doctor, the good doctor came, at long last. *Welcome, doctor, afternoon, sir, doctor, we have been looking for you, sir, doctor, we have got a really big emergency on our hands, doctor.* Mouths wagged disjointedly, all awash with the spittle of sycophancy. Big buttocks were rolling all over the stump of a man. The only response they got was a stern, studied stare. Perspiration was dripping from the armpits, face, nose, everywhere. The Stare was too busy striking down the rude buttocks to have time to wipe off the water washing his dirty body for the first time on that day.

Doc, we tried to get you over the phone, but it was dead. We even sent the driver to the house and madam said you had left very early and were supposed to be here at the hospital. Madam! Madam!! Madam!!! Nasty, old witch!!! She would never give him a break. She had been a thorn in his flesh for so long that he could not remember what it was to smile, not even when he was being joyfully smothered and suffocated in the gigantic arms of their house-girl who knew his plight and generously gave him of God's generous gift to her in the secluded room of an ex-patient living close to the cemetery. Madam! Madam!! Madam!!! She could not arouse the desire of Don Juan himself, so frigid was she, yet she would not stop locking the bedroom door and forcing him to sleep with her on a bed partitioned with her ice-cold backside. He had left home very early that morning, as usual, after she had brought him breakfast in bed at the instant when he was deep in the ecstasy of a wet dream. He awoke so suddenly that he knocked over the coffee pot in the tray and spilled the mess over his pajamas. He left in anger, without thinking of taking a wash.

Tests were taken on the three-year-old body. The Stare did not really need any test to conclude that the body needed blood transfusion, or another patient would be in the bed by the time he returned to duty the following day. The nursing sister instructed one of the staff nurses to start arrangements for the transfusion at once, but the Stare would not hear of it. The woman should have known better than to forget, or bypass, protocol and regulations: *You don't take out blood from the bank unless you replace it before you can take it out. You don't withdraw money from the bank unless you first save something, and you must know how much you have saved so as not to overdraw your account. Never write a check that will bounce, or you will be bounced into jail where you will rot until you die.*

And the three-year-old body lay there, still motionless, while they wrangled over regulations, and protocol, and emotion, and sympathy, and the bank, and blood that would flow too late. *I don't know you were so heartless! Imagine you reeling off all those nasty, meaningless rules when a boy lies there dying. Well, what do you want? Laws are laws, whether you are a king, or a cow. But, where is the boy's mother? I think she says she works somewhere. And his father, where is he? He has not come in at all? When your child is in the hospital, you ought to be there at his side, not running round wasting time, as if the poor thing didn't need you.*

Jimi was still on the other side of town, lying flat on his back, shot to shreds by the security guard of the tycoon abhorred by him and his friends. His blood, and that of his friends, had gushed out in large quantity, enough to fill the dry fountain at Independence Square, and had become dry, almost like the fountain in its post-independence element. It had colored the marble floor red, and was now dripping very slowly, and sporadically. One drop for a mother suffering from anemia at childbirth, and deprived of the God-given red liquid. One drop for a hard-luck plodder hit in his brand-new car on the very day of a purchase for which he had saved for a decade and had drunk coffee and soaked bread in it to survive, only to bleed to death at the back of an ambulance caught in a traffic-jam on the way to a hospital where there was no electric current to help the man keep a hold on life which he had more or less lost. One drop for a three-year-old already dead on his bed while those who matter are arguing over rules and regulations.

The battle was rather drawn out, an unexpected turn of events,

129

since the attackers were not aware that the big man had any guard in his mansion. The anticipated walk-over quickly became a war. Skirmish became siege, and darkness became dawn. Dawn gradually announced the death of all the intruders, Jimi being the last to fall.

Ten years of love, and hate, and love. Ten years of lies, and hypocrisy, and lies. Ten years of love and lies, and hate and hypocrisy. *I will always love you, only you, even when I'm dead and buried in my borrowed grave that will be acquired by the government from the man who stole it from my landlord and dug up so that they could erect the monument in honor of the national hero who sold us into modern slavery which must make you wonder about independence and development. You will always be in love with me when you spend your time poisoning me slowly and laughing at my decimated body while you spend fruitful time praying to the Almighty that I may live forever. I will forever be in love with you when I steal your love and sell it to the first bidder who pays me with a double lie which I bring back to you with elation in your lying face and in your body recently gyrating to the warmth of a lover who will soon kill you in your sleep. You will love me to death by sucking my breasts and my blood like a vampire unable to discriminate between friend and foe or the living and the dead.*

No one knew Jimi's whereabouts. The radio in the Stare's office, in the summary of the local news, mentioned a reported attack on the home of the most reputable son of the soil. Happily for the whole nation, so said the report, the heinous, unpatriotic attack by the nameless intruders was foiled by his alert, patriotic guards, and the dastardly criminals were lying there on the approaches to the house, for everyone to see. The Stare, a renowned pacifist, switched off the set. At home, his wife, also a pacifist, turned the set up a little louder, to better savor the occasion, and to hear other news about the triumph of the good and the trampling to death of the evil. *Goodness gracious me! Turn that damn thing down, will you? Can't you see it's too loud? Or, are you deaf, or something? Shut up, you...! But, I'm listening to the news, and you better take interest in these things, because you never know these days. Blood, blood, blood all over the place. I say, turn it down! Well, I won't. Come and do your worst, o. Oh, JT, you are simply a jive turkey, that is exactly what you are!!! Can't you understand? I say we must see to it that blood does not flow anymore in this dear, great nation of ours.*

And he was lying on the bed, waiting for his pint of blood which, according to the regulations, must not flow. The nursing sister suggested that they go and bring some vagabonds from the city square. They would willingly donate, for a pittance. *But, you cannot do that! Leave people's responsibility to them. This is a democracy, and you should let people decide how best to solve their problems.*

The Stare was fed up with the whole situation. He took his leave, and promised to return in the evening, although he was sure, they all were sure, that he was not coming back, that he would not be caught dead at that home of the dying and the dead, when he was supposed to be losing his umpteenth game of billiards at the den of his lawyer-friend.

Just after the Stare's departure, the nursing sister decided to use her initiative to save the boy's lost life. She ordered the workers to have everything ready for the transfusion. *You cannot wait on ceremony when a child's life is at stake. If they like, let them fire me, or give me a query, or take me to court.*

They set up the equipment. Blood -the bank had more than enough for a hundred people- was taken out. A pint of blood.

The nursing sister picked up the boy, all three years of him. He was dead.

Why are children born?

To bring happiness into the rotten lives of adults who know not what it is to be happy.

Why are children born?

To raise the hopes of hopeless people and bring them crashing to earth when they're least prepared for it.

But why are children born?

To transform the destiny of the downtrodden whose existence is definitively adapted to defeat and death.

But why are children born?

To serve as pawn in the hands of megalomaniacs dazzled by trash and treasuring dead and diseased objects of their love and hate.

But, tell me, why are children born?

To bring you hope to dash your hope for redemption when all you can redeem is your empty ego within a system that steals your very breath from you.

Tinu had spent a meaningless day at the office, and was hurrying to the hospital where her child lay cold and curled up in a bed shared with flies. *Oh, God, you cannot let my baby die!* She was running along the road, past other human problems hidden behind smiles of sorrow and happiness and hypocrisy and hate and harmony in a place they call a nation. Horns blared from vehicles controlled by reckless drivers driven by a death-wish. Human problems sauntered across red lights in a fog of sunlight on its way down to its resting place in the west. Feet were rushing and running, struggling, and shoving everything in sight, shuffling and strolling, in an encounter on that road to nowhere that they call Liberty. *Excuse me, can't you see that you are pushing me? Please, let me through, I am in a hurry to see my baby in the hospital.*

And, in some dark, public latrine, a tired body sat on the bowl letting out everything which had been weighing it down for only God knows how long. The pieces fell hard on a cockroach trying its best to escape the wrath of the explosive anus, and the murderous impact and odor of rotten food imprisoned for too long in an equally rotten body. *Oh, God, how can You do this to me? How! How! How! You son of a gun, are you blind, or what? Can you not see that a car is passing, or is it today that you have chosen to present your credentials to the devil?*

And in an office in the Secretariat, where files disappear by the score and unwary superior officers are eternally glued to their seats, a monger of intrigues and blackmail was searching the wastepaper-basket, only to dip his filthy fingers into the feces placed there by the enemy who was relaxing in his sitting-room and laughing to himself about the success of his practical joke. *Are you mad, laughing like that to yourself? I have told you that job of yours will make you crazy one day. Oh, God, if my baby dies, what shall I do?*

And the nursing crew had all the papers well prepared, the ones for the boy's admission, as well as those for his release. And he lay there on the bed, cold and curled up like a newly born in the womb, still safe from the woes of this damned world. Tinu rushed in, a crazy look on her face. She was heading for the bed, past the sea of relatives and friends there to celebrate the birth of another baby, or the birthday of a patient condemned to die on a hospital bed. At first, nobody noticed her. No one cared for her presence. She reached the bed, and realized that her baby had stopped breathing, for always. She picked him up, very slowly, and turned round to leave the home of death. *But you can't do that! Eh, woman, what are you up to? Don't you know that they are going to give him a pint of blood? And, there are hospital regulations, and procedures, and protocol, that must be followed to the letter, and you cannot disobey them.* A struggle ensued, naturally, between mother and caretakers of regulations and the Law in a lawless land where children die before they begin to live. *Oh, God, you have let my baby die, you have let him die, you have killed him!!! Woman, come here, come here, woman!!! What are you doing? You will kill her. You will kill him!!! Be careful, she may bite you, o. She is crazy, can't you see her eyes?*

Tinu walked silently past all those protesting mouths and bodies, out into the darkness of Liberty Road.

Black Gods

He was a simple, sad-looking man. We had never seen him before and, were it not for the words slavering out of his big, wide mouth, none of us would have noticed his presence. After all, slubberdegullion -wow! don't you think that is an exceptionally good word?- I mean, silly, slovenly bastards, are never welcome in this our great society. Nonetheless, as I say, he was an exception to the rule. He was dressed in a tattered, dark winter coat that must have been white a long time ago. The attire gave him the look of a ghost wading through snow under the grayish skies of a tropical country. And, yes, indeed, that makes you wonder... You should not, though, because I don't have to tell you that we are in Blafrica where winter coats are parts and parcel of our everyday wear under the scorching sun. Brother and sister, remember that we are civilized.

Well, there he was, hobbling along Independence Boulevard, which is a far better word than street, a rumpled piece of paper in his left hand, while the right, rather short and hairy, dangled lifelessly on his side.

"I have brought you all an important message from the Master," he intoned repeatedly, stopping and standing at attention as he finished the same strange sentence.

A few people, too busy seeking their fortune to care for such a dirty dog, shoved him off their path while they ran along, their feet hardly touching the ground, their heads in the clouds, their eyes glued to a goal impossible to imagine by common people such as you and I.

Such people with faraway goals were not a bother to the man with a message. He was now approaching the Square, trying hard to increase his pace, slobbering faster in conjunction with his walk. A crowd was following him. As they moved closer to the Square, they became more silent. Questions were being asked with their eyes. Bodies expressed unvoiced apprehension, and anxiety, and anguish.

Finally, they were at the Square. He hesitated for one second. He did not seem to know where exactly to stand, or sit. He needn't have done that; for, our people had placed him right at the center. They did not move very close to him. Another surprise, since we have always loved the closeness of the human body, at any time, at any place, in any form.

Silence! You always talk too much, you useless man. Why can't you give your fellow man a chance to voice his opinion? After all, this is a Democracy, a haven of our demonstrative people, a mockery of the departed Master, a crazy combination of races. Black and Brown. Arabs and Africans. Niggers and Niggards. Whites and Whores. Yes, a Democracy, and that man has as much right as you or anyone else. So also do I. Another thing that bothers me about you: You never stop thinking of women. Remember? We were there at the Square, onlookers at an interesting spectacle, witnesses to a great event, and yet all you wanted to do was talk about that woman's figure. You even had the temerity to touch her once, and I had told you to lay off, you black... Yes, I know, I know, I said that she was my sister. Of course, she is my sister, she was and will forever be my sister. It doesn't matter. Just forget about her, and be serious for one minute, all right?

He was looking at each and every face in the wide circle surrounding him. His Adam's apple was dancing up and down as if to the beat of *fuji*, the latest craze among our country's majority of merrymakers. And, yes, *fuji* makes me think of fugitive, I mean, all those trying desperately to escape from our great nation. *All right, I realize that I am digressing from the real story. I know you are anxious to hear the strange tale.* I had not noticed before, but the man was sweating profusely under his winter coat. He did not take time to wipe away the sweat. For just an instant, my mind went back to our house near the dam. Our house built many years ago. Our house which had always enjoyed the advantage of running tap-water. Then came Independence and the Dam, with promises of greater things to come, including an abrupt end to our water-supply. Surely, I was not alone in thinking of water at the sight of that tattered body bathed in sweat. The man next to me kept licking his dry lips with his tongue, like a snake ogling an unwary prey. Another had his mouth wide open, as if he was waiting for a tap to open up and fill his toothless cavity. A third never stopped looking at the skies. Indeed, clouds were beginning to gather. Some were curled in circles in variegated colors. Some were moving like the multitude of patriots that usually follow the limousine of our dear President in his monthly meet-the-masses ride through the capital city. Perhaps the rain was the man's special message from the person whom he called the Master. Perhaps the poor were to be purged of their poverty. Perhaps the gadgets imported after Independence were going to start working. Perhaps death and destruction and decadence were going to die. Perhaps heaven was going to come down to earth, instead of people having to wait forever to taste of it after they have become carcasses.

"I have brought you an important message from the Master." The eyes suddenly became peaceful. They no longer wandered from one black face to another. The black faces themselves were suddenly rid of their questioning, or confusion. Harmony between messenger and masses. Understanding between brothers and sisters. Unity between stranger and the children of God. He opened the rumpled paper in his hand, took out a pair of glasses from his pocket, and read out loud, without a stutter:

"The Master has decreed that, for one whole week, His black children shall rule the world."

Just as abruptly as it had appeared, serenity disappeared from those nameless faces. Questions returned. Discrimination came back to life. Big eyes wandered to and fro, seeking answers where they did not exist, from other eyes seeking solace from everywhere and nowhere. Confusion set in. Feet imprisoned in torn, imported shoes shuffled in disarray on the disintegrating slabs of Independence Square. Some feet approached the Master's messenger, not in unison, not with any specific objective, although one could read a certain fear in the man's eyes. Others moved away, further away, only to turn round and walk briskly, and menacingly, towards the tattered center of attraction. One individual, he must be in his mid-twenties, spat out a curse while farting long and loud to the amusement of the astonished crowd. The odor spread so fast that they all covered their noses with their hands and ran for shelter, as if a bomb was dropping from the skies. But, naturally, no shelter worth the name was available for miles around. Besides, how on earth does one hide from an odor? The buildings, mostly government and company offices, tall, menacing concrete staring down on the ant-like black bodies, were all locked up. The gutters, yawning crevices filled with filth that must have accumulated from the very day the National Anthem was sung, and the new flag raised, lay across from the Square. A few people ran towards them, but they were forced to scuttle back as the stench welcoming them had a more repulsive scent than the one from which they were trying to flee.

Come on now, you! Don't remind me of things I would rather forget. I know, cheating is unpatriotic. One is expected to steal openly, to be proud of it, proclaim it to the whole wide world, and calmly declare one's innocence. The cheat must be punished for his pettiness, for his attempt to reduce our great nation to the level of a small-time crook, when onlookers expect from us grand designs and great deeds. So, I shall tell you the whole story, I shall not cheat, I shall let them know everything, if and since that is what you want. I shall shelve the idea of displaying my nationalism and patriotism until another occasion when I can do it in a big way. And you may rest assured that I shall be a big-time crook, a true son of this rich soil of ours.

The rush for the gutters by those cowardly fools was sudden, as I have already stated. Among them was a small boy, about five years old, clinging to the receding hand of a man who must be his father. The latter was in such a haste to escape that he was paying no attention to the desperate brat impeding his progress. Now, what was a child doing among that crowd? *These children, they are so hard-headed, so nosy, that they'd wish to outdo the adults in the game of life.* The man was right to let go of the brat's hand, right there in the middle of the road circling the Square, right in the path of a late-model car raising a cloud of dust and blaring the sweet music of custom-made horns proclaiming the owner's genius for stealing the nation blind. Yes, indeed, the man let go of the boy's hand, jumped barely clear of the oncoming vehicle, and landed in the gutter, to take a filthy bath that he really needed. The boy's mouth was agape at the simultaneous loss of the guiding hand and the marriage of his willowy frame to the sleek, inviting body of the speeding car. The car did not stop. It ran over the frail human body. The driver did not even realize that his flying vehicle had hit anything. The spectators were too busy taking care of business to waste time on the fallen body. A few glances and a sigh of anguish, here and there. The message had to be deciphered, the odor had to be conquered, and only a fool would waste precious time attending to a dead body, particularly to the body of a child.

unmatched in our whole nation. Female employees of NTB changed last names as they changed clothes. Men had black eyes as often as human punch-bags at the receiving end of a champion boxer's sharp left jabs. Turn-over, female turn-over, in particular, was as rampant as the nightly power failure in our progressive capital city. And Mr. President, a man who had traveled far and wide, with exact information on the best hotels in the world's capitals well kept in his left hand, Mr. President never stopped boasting of the television company's exemplar, nor did he tire of advising sister organizations to emulate the National Electricity Corporation (NEC) with its reputation for incompetence. His zeal was quite understandable: He had taken four of his dear wives from both highly reputed establishments. Naturally, he had exercised the wisdom of equality by taking two from each place.

Upon arrival at the television station, he was led by the inebriated Manager to the Press Center. The official scurried to the near-by NEC building and, in a jiffy, the whole station was bathed in light. A real heaven, indeed, surrounded by an endless stretch of darkness that one would call hell. Such darkness did not matter. If Mr. President could make his speech, the home audience did not have to listen, or watch. The handful of officials on the spot was enough to pass on the message to the others elsewhere.

"His Excellency, Honorable Chief Doctor Robinson Immanuel Prospero, the one and only Life President of our dearly beloved nation, the Messiah, our Father, a man of steel, a man among boys, a descendant of slaves returned home to his roots, to lead Africa out of the wilderness to the land of plenty and power, a classmate of other descendants of slaves in Blamerica, a friend of descendants of slave-owners whom, by means of his charm and civilized manners, he has turned into humble human beings, a lover of children and of their mothers, the head of a great family, and so on and so forth, *ad infinitum*, is here to speak to us tonight."

The speaker of those simple and straightforward words, was the NTB Manager, a relation of Mr. President's and a recent returnee from some unspecified foreign country where he had spent the greater part of his forty odd years without achieving anything more than the invaluable experience of living among civilized folks.

The Messiah himself sat with that grin fixed on his face. While he was being introduced, he fidgeted with his tie which seemed on the point of flying off his neck. He constantly cleared his hardly visible throat. Then came his turn to perform miracles with words.

"Ladies and gentlemen, compatriots and dear foreign brothers and sisters, adults and children, especially children, and all the other combi..."

All of a sudden, the lights went out. The Manager swore out loud and promised to cut off the mammary glands of the mother of the NEC boss. As he was rolling towards the courtyard, falling over several things on the way, someone shouted the good news to him: Power had been restored. He heaved a sigh of relief and lumbered back toward the Press Center.

"As I was saying before the gods took away the electricity, my most sincere greetings of love go to the children, and all other combinations of our dear land. Before I continue, let me comment on this event that we just witnessed, I mean the lights out. Let us be very clear about it. We are being tested by God, and the gods. They are warning us against evil. They are telling us to change our evil ways; or else, they might decide to condemn us to darkness everlasting. Just think about it. Had it not been for our patriotic staff here, led by our humble selves, that light would never have come back. Praise be to the Almighty; my people, let us praise our Great Lord."

The applause, already recorded on tape, drowned out any effort that the handful of witnesses could muster to make Mr. President feel good. He was quite pleased with himself. He thrust forward his chest, and continued:

"Well, I am here to announce to you the dawn of a new day, a day that will last one whole week, the week of black supremacy. So as not to waste your precious time..."

Again, suddenly, the gods, and God, decreed darkness. Mr. President was not at all bothered. He simply continued talking:

"...let me give you an outline of our program. First, I am sending out emissaries tomorrow to import slaves, precisely, white slaves from overseas to work on our farms and in our factories. Messages will be taken to our brothers and sisters in Blamerica, Blantilla, Boomland, and Queensland, to ask for their delegations to a top-notch meeting here in our great nation, to decide on an international program for all of the Black Race. An Executive Council meeting has been called for this very night, to choose the emissaries and to take other far-reaching decisions. During this week of our supremacy, the number of days will be changed to eight, so that four days will be used to work, and the other four for rest. This, you would agree, is a matter of equality. Our great nation has worked so hard for so long, that now is the time to take our well-deserved rest. With regards to the overall condition in this great nation of ours, I hereby decree that all those females who are yellow, pink, or white, be seized at once. They are to be placed in special breeding houses. Our great national Army, docile and useless since its creation at Independence, will now be made to exercise their great striking power. The men are to be locked up throughout the week, with those women. For both parties, the eight-day week will be enforced, especially as they will be engaged in services to humanity. Regarding all the other male citizens over fourteen, each of them is to immediately take five women of his choice. Ours is a nation of love, of harmony, of collective action. I note that the ratio of females to males at and above the age specified is five to one. We do not want our women to suffer, nor do we want our men, the young ones inclusive, to be wayward. Remember this is our opportunity to prove to the whole world our human quality. To exemplify that quality, I have decided myself to take a seventh wife. I would have taken two more, to make eight in accordance with the new decree about the eight-day week, but in my humility and in adherence to the time-honored tradition of the Master, I shall stop at seven, at least for now. In order to bring into reality the element of prosperity of this great nation, every citizen is to be given a car as soon as the new slaves arrive to construct new vehicles. Other decisions will be made known to you all when they have been taken by me, your dear Messiah. Meanwhile, anyone contravening any of the above decrees will be seriously dealt with. Let me again remind you all that this is a momentous minute. Our reputation is at stake, and we must not fail the Almighty and our very selves. To ensure the total success of our program, I shall instruct the Police to take into protective custody certain individuals whose presence among our patriotic people will jeopardize not only the survival of the people but also our national existence, as well as their own very lives. Long live Blafrica, and God bless you all!"

The lights were still out. Mr. President was no doubt a genius. He had not read a single line of his glorious speech, he had not even prepared anything; yet he spoke so precisely, so intelligently, so brilliantly, so convincingly. Just as he was beginning to wonder what to do next - clear his throat one more time? begin another speech? or what?- electricity was restored. To his utter surprise, the room was deserted. Fear gripped him by the throat; he was literally about to choke. *Those bastards! They think they can stop the wheels of progress from progressing. They think they can disobey the Master by frustrating the noble efforts of the Messiah. We shall see what they are up to pretty soon. We shall see who is in charge. He who laughs last, laughs last! We shall soon see the best laugher. If no one reappears in a minute, there will be serious trouble for this whole nation!!!*

No one showed his face for a long half-hour. Nothing happened to the room, and the nation remained what it always was, a conglomeration of heterogeneous groups joined together by only one noble characteristic, that of prostitution in all its forms. And Mr. President sat there trying not to choke. He knew, rather, he hoped, that nothing bad would befall him. He was already planning another speech to placate those whom he had probably offended by the earlier outburst. Poor him! After all, he loved the nation so much, he had served her so fervently, so devotedly, that it had rewarded him with the right to own its best human and material products. Everybody knew that his wives were among the prettiest creatures ever seen in the whole world. He also owned millions of the nation's money in foreign banks, as well as a few summer hideaways, no doubt all with the consent of his dear compatriots or, rather, children. He was definitely the best thing that ever happened to Blafrica. The people must agree with him. The children, too. As a symbol of their love for him, his pictures graced every visible public space in the nation. Moreover, children sang a hymn in his honor every morning at school assembly. Government employees, not to be outdone, swore allegiance to him once a week. And now, this opportunity, this singular opportunity to broaden the scope of his already legitimate, authentic supremacy...

A side-door opened very gently, and his chauffeur, one of the score at his disposal, stuck in his ostrich-like neck. The man was dripping wet like a swimmer fresh out of the pool. He looked from side to side in the manner of a thief almost cornered by the scrupulous arm of the law. Once sure of his safety, he tip-toed to center-stage, approaching the great Mr. President, and whispered in his ear. The Messiah, pleased with what he heard, let go a belly-laugh that echoed yards away, stood his whole short length, stretched with pride and reassurance, and strolled majestically out into the courtyard.

How dare anybody in his right mind think of harming the great Mr. President? Particularly at that moment of great events in the life of our dear, great nation? The Messiah jumped into his limo. He ordered the fretful colossus of a chauffeur to step on it, because he had to meet the Executive Council at the palace. Of course, the colossus obeyed. He was traveling as fast as the wind. He went through red traffic lights with impunity. Zebra crossings, almost obliterated by dirty feet, did not even exist in the man's mind. Pedestrians, vehicles, anything and anyone at all, belonged to another world. He had been given a license to kill by Mr. President himself, and it was a miracle that he did not leave any dead bodies in his wake.

At the palace, the Council had congregated in the Executive Chambers, waiting respectfully for Mr. President over assorted imported liquor served by charming teenage girls specially engaged to entertain the highest servants of our dear nation. When one of the girls announced Mr. President's arrival, there was general grumbling among the ruling servants of the nation. They still had enough patience to last the whole night, so he might have taken his time, instead of rushing back. They understood the particular nature of his post, they sympathized with him most sincerely, and they did not want him to have hypertension running all over the place.

Mr. President came in to a standing ovation masterfully choreographed by his second-in-command, the Honorable Minister of Finance, Defense, Justice, and Social Affairs. He was definitely tired - running our great nation could not be easy, must not be easy, no way!- and everyone hoped that the meeting would be brief, so that Mr. President could retire and his henchmen could finish their drinks in company of the fine teenagers.

Indeed, it was a whirlwind affair. Mr. President designated people to fly out to the various nations the following day, for consultation over the Master's message. Representatives from Blamerica, Blantilla, Boomland, and Queensland, all nations with vast populations of blacks, coloreds, negroes, quarterons, mulattoes, niggers, were to be invited to visit Blafrica for serious, heart-to-heart discussions on the destiny of the Race, and the universe. A group of specialists in inhuman affairs would go to buy white slaves for various essential services in the nation.

＊　　＊　　＊

The following day, the whole capital was in turmoil. News of arrests was spreading like wildfire. The prisons were overfilled with intellectuals whose continued presence among the general populace was deemed prejudicial not only to the survival of their fellow men, but also to our national existence and, in particular, to their own lives.

Stop bothering me, you! Yes, I know that your dear brother was one of the unfortunate guests of the nation, and that your poor mother died of the anguish. But you must have forgotten that stories made the round in intellectual circles that your mother was destined to die, anyway, for that set of human skulls discovered in her bedroom by our colleague at college, I mean, your ugly sister's boyfriend... Come now, don't be angry, I am just trying to set the record straight, and you will agree with me that all angles of a story should be carefully examined before a final opinion is made. Well, forget what I said about your mother. You say what? There you go again, trying to be difficult. So, what if what is said can never be unsaid? So, what if I meant every word of what I said? What do you want of me, anyway? To go searching for my words in the wind, and eat them up? To beg the Almighty to make people forget that I ever said them? You should remember — are you not a true son of the soil? — that we all have short memories here, most especially as regards the truth. And since the truth about you and your mother is symbolic of that which is hidden in the nooks and crannies of many other lives, why do you have to worry? Besides... I heard you saying something just now... Eh, stop it! Why are you alluding again to my pretty sister's backside? She is far too good for the likes of you. You are too black, too big, too bush!!! I am going to marry her off to a rich, civilized doctor of letters and license, who will take good care of her. So, forget about her, and her backside. You think I should go back abroad? But, what brought that weird notion to your head? Well, well, what do you know? Here I am being implored by my best friend to leave my own home. Let me tell you, dear friend, dear brother, dearer father, dearest mother and sister, all of you who usually listen by blocking your ears in order not to hear, let me tell you that we shall all stay here together. It is our right to share the national cake, even if it is cankered. It is our duty to contribute our quota, be it corrupt or corruptible, to make this great

146

nation gross, not great. It is our absolute right to savage this nation and send it into ruination. It is our privilege to feed fat on our fatherland's food, even if the poor have to starve to death to provide for our needs. No sacrifice can ever be too much for the well-being of the nation's elite.

Now, that was the mistake made by our dear Mr. President that fateful week. The man simply underestimated the potency of the human brain. By placing the intellectuals in what he called protective custody, he set in motion the machinery that would nullify the very progress that he claimed to be seeking. He did not understand that our people, may the Almighty bless their sweet souls, have always revered knowledge. Just by reminding the criminals in jail of their beautiful alphabetic combinations of degrees, from A to Z, the newly-arrived prisoners were guaranteed a riot of unfathomable proportions.

Another awe-inspiring aspect of their sojourn in prison, was the very intelligent, incomprehensible declamation of one of their number, an elderly recent returnee from Blamerica where, according to what he told his friends and the wide-eyed bunch of criminals in attendance, he used to be Mr. President's classmate. He regaled them with his interesting revelations:

"The guy has always been known for his autocratic, dictatorial, oppressive, inhuman, and barbarian manners. I was convinced long ago that he would love to winnow out the grain to cuddle the shaft of the nation's human resources. Pity, my brothers, pity. Pity, pity a million times! Pity, my sisters in absentia, pity. But, I can assure you, we shall overcome, I do know that we *will* overcome some day."

◈   ◈   ◈

In the capital city of Blamerica, the announcement of the one-week black rule of glory was made on the same day as in Blafrica. However, in the former haven on earth, it took place in the evening, on television. Immediately, there was a blackout, the very first in almost a century. The announcer -a man whose tegumentary condition was impossible to determine what with the abruptness of the announcement, the snow on all sets at that very instant and, particularly, the mask covering his face- spoke only half-seriously. Nobody paid attention to that, though. Before you could say, "we shall overcome," the streets of Cadillac City were flooded with rejoicing blacks of all shades and sizes.

"Eh, man, this is like wow! I'm gonna get me a honkey and beat the hell outta the mothah."

"Gee weez, ain't that a shit? Seems like God's wakin' up after all them years of slumber. But y'all know som'? I du know, you can't ever trust these goddamn whiteys. You think they mean som', and you find out quick enough it's no damn thang!"

"But, man, that can't be true. See, this ain't never took place before, so it can't be no lie. Whatever it be, I'm gonna have ma fun right now! And you, too, brotha. Better git off your ass and do som'. You got just one week, man, just one lousy week!"

"Eh, sistah, let's go booogie! They say the Man done set us freeee for one whole week! All I need is a hog, some good root beer, a reefer, a real bad mama, and an island in the sun."

"Me, I jes wanna go back hum to Africa. Take me away to Africa, ma hum, Africa, ma heart, Africa, ma honey, Africa, ma all!!!"

"And Africa your hell, brother! To hell with all them Africa talk! The guys ain't shit. They're too damn proud, all of them, too damn crazy. Too damn conniving with them white folk, they make me sick! Matter of fact, I'd rather git me a nigger from the jungle, and piss on his savage face, than spit on the face of a honkey."

Among the crowd turning round in circles was Caliban-Mason-Dixon-King, reputed leader of a ghetto gang. An orphan who did not know his father and whose mother was lynched by a white mob for refusing to sit at the back of an almost empty bus, he grew up in no particular place. He shared his early life between his blind maternal grandmother, his paralyzed paternal aunt, a neighborhood pastor whose special vocation was, giving succor to the growing community of those in search of sexual liberation, and a white convict he met in prison who taught him the essential means of survival in a wicked world. That he lived to be ten was a wonder only God could explain. That he survived to be twenty-one was a miracle. That he would go on till thirty was inconceivable. King lived virtually on the edge of a precipice into which he showed signs of tumbling every day. Yet, somehow, he stayed out of it, with his wide grin, his lackadaisical manner, his thick-lens glasses, and his Bible.

Yes, a Bible, and that used to astonish all his acquaintances no end. On that fateful night of legalized black rule, King was moving among his confused crowd, reflecting on what he had heard on a friend's TV, trying to decide on how exactly he could positively use the week of glory. Go on a shooting spree to avenge his race? Take a satellite and head for a short stay on the moon? Pick up all the things he had always wanted but would never have? Such ideas were excellent, he thought, but there was still something lacking in them. Then, the best notion came to him like the sun emerging at midnight: He would summon his friends, go occupy the White House, the presidential residence, and rule the country for that glorious week.

What a gem of an idea! What a genius he was! He had always known it, there was definitely a long line of kings, princes, and great warriors in his ancestry. He remembered his grandmother's stories about how his forefathers had crossed the great seas in warships to conquer Blamerica; how, unfortunately, their ship had capsized and how, with supreme efforts of courage and endurance, they had managed to reach land where some white crooks had enslaved them. But now, there he was, the descendant of great men, resuscitating the dormant atavistic qualities of the family. He would be the president, a great president, the great president; he might even change the damn government into a monarchy, because that would blend marvelously with his background.

He wended his way through the milling crowd, casting a glance here and there, calling out names, heading for the ghetto, his ghetto.

The journey was not easy, however. The confused crowd appeared to have a common objective in mind, although nobody ever said a word about it. The reality of days on end without a meal. The truth of a life without a purpose, without a past, without possibilities. The gnawing presence of death. The feeling that despondency and desolation were too heavy on minds that might soon go mad. The thought of one action, just one action, one telling blow, struck against the murderous System.

The circles were growing visibly wider. The elation of the first moments was transmuting into impatience. The conversations were becoming somewhat desperate.

"Lord, what am I gonna do? They tell us we are free, that we are kings, but they don't tell us what to do. Why?"

"Niggers of the world, arise! Rejoice in the name of the Race! Let freedom reign!"

"Hallelujah!"

"What is happening, blood? Ain't som' odd 'bout all this jive talk about freedom? I don't see no freedom, d'ya?"

"Where the hell we headin' foh?"

"I wanna go hum, man, I'm tired, let me be, huh! I don't wan no nigger telling me what to do!"

The desperation of the present mixed with the cynicism of the past. Past and present projected into a future of lost promises. The multitude kept moving, apparently in circles, but really in a direction where power, that is, wealth, had its abode. The First Union Bank, Uncle Tom's Jewelry Stores, Steinberg's, and Billboard, Inc., among others, all well-established, all successful, all housed in the imposing skyscrapers of Main Street overlooking the Den, the largest ghetto in Blamerica, lay within easy reach of that confused sea of human bodies. And the blacks, forever in search of Civilization, had for long constituted the major clientele of those pocket-cleaning enterprises. Indeed, inhabitants of the Den often discussed why the ghetto was so close to Main Street. Various answers were suggested but, in the final analysis, they were secondary to the whole issue. Whatever explanation there was, the fact remained, that Main Street attracted blacks and would continue to do so, because it gave them what their hearts yearned for: material, and the means to purchase it. Easy credit, and endless debts. Pay cash and carry, but also unload, use, and pay later, or never.

Window-shopping was the hobby of ghetto dwellers. And, as years passed by, the hobby became a desperate habit; for, the credit system was feeling the crunch of debtors departing from the scene without paying a penny. Shopping with one's eyes thus came to serve not only as a panacea for poverty but, more and more, as a poison to the pauper. A few burglary attempts had lately been reported. The ill-advised effort naturally resulted in arrest and long jail-terms. By reputation, the guards on Main Street, mainly ex-servicemen armed with machine guns and aided by Dobermans, were experts in maintaining law and order. They worked day and night, twenty-four hours a day, seven days a week. They rotated their vacation. King and his friends had given them a perfect name: *the Mean Machine of Main Street* or, more simply put, *the Three M's.*

On that Black Night -but, who could ever have imagined it?- the three M's and their pinschers were nowhere to be found. A civilized machine breaking down? A hen growing teeth? The devil taking a nap? You betcha life it ain't so!

"But, where them bastards guarding the green paradise?"

"Eh, man, them busters don go to sleep for the first time in history. Shiiit! They really gone to sleep!!!"

"Good God Almighty!!! Blood, som' tells me we're gonna really overcome tonight."

Suddenly, the lights returned to life. Mellifluous voices swept back and forth, as rhythmically as the jazzy melodies of the inspired choir and congregation on a holy day. The first reaction to the light was an attempt to hide; but that was only momentary. They were now right there on Main Street, there by accident, or design, there in the middle of the almighty material of the earthly masters, there by the power of the Master who had just liberated them from their shackles. Eyes were ogling the pretty jewelry. Minds were imagining the wretched bodies clad in beautiful clothes, the extra-large feet squeezed into the latest shoes, and empty pockets inflated with uncountable money-bills.

King, too, was there. He had seen only six of his gang and was searching for another six. The first six had been instructed to go to the dilapidated building at the corner of the Den, the place that used to be a beer-parlor frequented by the best women, and serving the best wine, until fire razed it to the ground one hot, summer day. King did not really want to be on Main Street. He was so anxious to put into practice his lofty notion that he wished the crowd did not exist, that only his remaining six disciples were there on the street. Not that he minded taking another peek at the expensive silk suit he had been planning to buy for over six months. But the suit and other goodies would be there long after his one-week stint in the White House had entered Blamerican lore. Or, would they?

There he was in front of Steinberg's, staring at the silk suit. Something snapped inside him. He flung his Bible at the glass before him and, almost simultaneously, he dived after it. He landed in a heap among a cluster of clothing. His action was a sort of signal to others gaping through the windows at a world of gorgeous dresses. It was as if the flood-gates of a dam had burst open, unexpectedly. Fiery looks turned into hysterical gazes. Feet with nowhere to go found a destination in a hurry. Dreams became reality.

In the twinkling of an eye, the peaceful world of Main Street's white stores was transformed into a universe of black dream-makers. People took everything, and anything. King was wearing his silk suit, half-torn, and smeared with blood, a peevish grin glued to his ebony face. Shoving and sliding, he was calling out to his still unfound followers. Somehow, he had succeeded in keeping his glasses on his face, and in retrieving his Bible from the heap of clothes and shattered glass. He was holding aloft the Word of the Almighty and, for a long second, he resembled the Messiah there to save His people and lead them to the land of honey and money.

Then, the place was lit up in flames and smoke. All the stores were on fire, including the First Union Bank. Heaven became one with hell. Black came into sudden harmony with white.

"Praise the Lord, praise the living Lord! Today oughtta be Judgment Day."

"You kin say that agin, man! The whole worl's a-comin' to an end."

"Eh, mama, help me with this stuff here. I gotta catch me the playoffs on this sweet li' box next week."

"Mama, maaaama! Where's you at, ma? Please, take me to mah mama!"

The little boy's cry was not an exception in that motley crowd. Indeed, there must have been as many children as adults on Main Street. After all, little ones need to survive as much as grown-ups. And the wise have always said the kids have more rights than the old Uncle Toms who are standing steps away from their six-foot deep underground home.

King took one of the kids by the arm and led him away, in the direction of the Den. The boy was going to serve as his mascot in the White House. Just like them honkey kings ruling their vast kingdoms, the ones his teacher used to talk so much about, disturbing King's peaceful sleep after a hard night on the streets. Of course, there was no way he was going to stick that shit for more than a few days.

What was going down on Main Street was, to King's mind, already a significant part of history. The history of a Civilization in which the law of the jungle prevailed. Destroy before you are destroyed. Give nothing and take everything. Blessed are the selfish, and the shifty, and the crooked, and the cheats, and the prostitutes, and their pimps; for, they all shall inherit the kingdom of this democratic earth, just as the enslavers have magnificently proved it. And, images of Democracy flashed across the man's crowded and clouded mind.

The mad bomber calling on the phone to tell the police of bombs placed in various hot spots in Cadillac City -stores, hospitals, theatres, playgrounds- turned out to be an orphaned eight-year-old claiming to be in search of his parents and God.

A man and a woman, once lovers, once married to each other, but now divorced for some fifteen years, decided to reconcile, and their first act of reconciliation was to go to the foster-home of their only son, given away twenty years before, to take him with them at gun-point. They were so much in love with him that they could not live another second without him by their side.

A woman and her man-friend wrapped up the former's two children, two and three years of age respectively, and set them on fire. They then reported to the authorities that the kids had been kidnapped. When the truth came out, they swore that their real intention was, to leave the sinful world behind, become totally celibate, and give their lives to God and His work.

A final-year, first-class student in Cadillac University climbed to the top of the tower at the center of campus, and gunned down fifty colleagues and professors with a telescopic rifle. Before they could catch him, he swallowed a bullet, and left a note stating with good reason: "This is a crazy world."

A rich philanthropist kept a lion in his backyard. The thoroughly domesticated beast broke loose one sunny day, and killed three children in the bourgeois neighborhood. Police could not file any charges against the man: There was no law against keeping pets and, besides, the guy was such a nice citizen recognized for his magnanimity.

Nice persons were hard to come by in Blamerica, and King was determined to change the situation. Democracy, the word kept ringing in his skull. He would democratize the whole world; he would democratize women; he would democratize children; he would democratize men; he would democratize Democracy!!!

Before the night ended, he had found all the members of his entourage. At the break of day, they headed for the White House. The mansion was empty except for the negro servants that used to work for the white president. *Good God Almighty*! The place was damn too large for one person and his family. King's first act as national overlord was to instruct a couple of his disciples to return to the Den and invite as many women as possible to come live with him. After all, he needed a wife; and women, according to tales recounted by his grandmother, had always been the pillar behind men in black society. In next to no time at all, a bevy of black beauties arrived in the White House. However, Caliban Mason-Dixon King became mad at that sea of black faces.

"Racism," he intoned, "has gotta be stamped out, and we gonna start right here. The good Book teaches us not to take an eye for an eye. The fact that them whiteys made a mistake does not mean we gotta follow their bad example. We wanna start something new on this earth!"

Power changes, power transforms, power reveals. King the ghetto boy, King the rabble-rouser, King the nigger, was no more! The man - even his speech was becoming rather different- was now preaching a brand of humanism that surprised even his twelve disciples who had seen him perform surgery on skulls before, and that with the Good Book clutched in his big hands. The racists who had gone to recruit just negro women were summarily dismissed and sent back to the Den never again to catch a glimpse of the White House as long as King was in control. He detailed other people to go in search of white women, wine-colored women, chestnut-colored women, coffee-colored women, all-sorts-of-colored women. From among that United Colors of Women, the new president would choose a spouse.

Meanwhile, King's policy of humanizing the races and the ranks, was rendered untenable by the total absence of white men. Where on earth could they be? They, the once too visible masters of the universe. They, the too assertive controllers of black destiny in the ever-present past. They, the too well recognized leaders of society just the day before. King sent some disciples to fish them out of their hiding place. They were to be pampered, and patronized; but, in case that failed, he threatened to change his policy, and enslave them. For him, one thing was certain: Whites must be part of the new society. They were needed in Cadillac City, to lend their legendary expertise to the manufacture of cars. Moreover, their attention would be useful in the general running of state affairs, since they were so experienced in such things. King was hoping and praying that they would be found, and soonest. He wanted very much to prove to them that the negro was love, that the negro was life, that the negro was a king, and wonderfully egalitarian overlord.

In the afternoon, a nationally televised statement was read by Mr. President King. The scene was reminiscent of earlier times, just the day before, with the one exception that the all-white screen had become all-black. Every aspect of the show was well coordinated, and everything went without a hitch. King's speech was excellent, and the live audience applauded every word, every movement of his mouth, and even the batting of his eye, the picking of his nose, the superficial cough, the odd sneeze borrowed from the civilized masters. Another difference, perhaps not of much significance, was the special exclamations and declamations used in applauding the speech. No white audience could have matched the zeal, the flavor, indeed, the soul of King's admiring listeners, as hallelujahs and yes-lords filled the air.

"And..."

"Yes, Lord!"

"...there will be love and prosperity in this nation of ours."

"Say it, say it!!!"

"And black and white will live in harmony for this one, glorious week."

"Hallelujah!"

"And we shall all be freeeeeeee!!!"

"Keep talking, you talking now!"

"And, as I am speaking to you right now, arrangements are being made to contact our brothers in Blafrica, and in Blantilla, in all them funny places where other blacks live, to seek ways in which we all can benefit, together, from this week of profound significance."

"Tell them, brother, tell them!"

"Hmm..."

"Hurrah for all the brothers of the world!!!"

"I have sent my disciples to bring the white brothers out of their hiding place. We wanna let them know at this time, that we don't hate nobadeeeee! We love them, we wanna embrace them, to hold them close to our warm hearts, we want them to cooperate with us because, without pulling together *all* our forces, we can never ever achieve anything."

"Good God in heaven! The man be talking!!!"

Caliban Mason-Dixon King was truly inspired. Unfortunately, he had no chance to fully display his gift of the gab. A snub-nosed man suddenly emerged from the shadows, and whispered into his ear. The speech was over. Without saying another word to his captivated audience, Mr. President practically ran from the podium. He left the cameramen to focus their attention on the gyrating backside of the multi-colored female visitors. Three disciples followed him. They all went into an adjoining room where some men were waiting for the president.

The visitors were from Blafrica, although from the way King and his men were staring at them, one would have mistaken them for intruders from another planet. In truth, the blacks from the New World had met some of them before, but the latter, frequent callers at Uncle LeRoi's, the most popular hide-out in the Den, had become quite civilized, quite adapted to life in modern society. Hearing them engage in their loud conversation in impeccable English, you would not believe that some of them came from those faraway lands where folk spoke strange languages.

"They be gittin' down and gittin' up, slappin' dem fingahs, givin' n' takin' fives, messin' around with them women and stuff."

Of course, they used to wear their native attire, but nothing resembling the flowing, over-sized pajamas worn by the new arrivals. And, those newcomers were wearing coats on top of everything else.

For their part, the Blafricans were simply too pleased to be in Cadillac City, in the White House in particular, to bother about the impression they gave their guests. Grinning from ear to ear, revealing teeth caked over with remnants of food zealously devoured on the plane, they shook hands with their newly found brothers, hugged them, and squeezed them to their hearts. King's mind fleetingly painted pictures of humanoids from another world, but the touch of their bodies dispelled that notion.

Drinks were served.

"Wow! Can these guys drink! They are worse than fish. And, to think those winos at the corner of L and M Streets are bad..."

Then came lunch.

"Lordy, Lordy! They must have come starving all the way from their country."

Robinson Immanuel Prospero's emissaries, eminent gentlemen all, led by the honorable Minister of Finance, Defense, Justice, and Social Affairs, Fineface English Oniya, over-ate and over-drank. They ogled the multicolored women serving them, touched some backsides hanging in the way of their hyper-active hands, and demanded to own what they saw and touched. However, that desire had to wait until the urgent issue of the Race's destiny was discussed.

President King gradually warmed to his strange visitors. He now considered them and those they were representing as important branches of the Blamerican tree, and instruments to be used in disseminating Democracy among the backward peoples of the yet-to-develop world. He naturally felt insulted that their man had the temerity to invite him to their country. He decided to honor the invitation, all the same, by sending a high-powered delegation, since it would also afford him the opportunity to see through the eyes of those like him, the land from which his fortunate ancestors had been sold into Civilization.

Fineface English Oniya had no doubt made a remarkable speech. Its impact upon the audience was noticeable: Eyes and mouths were opened so wide that lips and lids almost met, just like earth and sky!

"Our own dear, honorable, revered, God-fearing, omnipotent, omnihuman, omnific, dear Mr. President, I should remind us, was trained in this country, in this great Democracy. During his sojourn here, he revealed his magnanimity, his potentiality, his incomparability in each and every aspect of life. Symbolic and symptomatic of his quality is the state of our nation today. His humanism has engrossed all of our people, and it is our fervent hope that all you our brothers and, of course, our dear sisters, too, will come to partake of the unparalleled qualities oozing from every pore of the great man's body. Today, we in our nation have conquered that notoriously implacable enemy of man, War, and its son, Death. Our emphasis is on Life. We make wives, not war, and we make babies, not bombs. Do forgive the genial language."

The audience erupted in loud, prolonged applause while Oniya continued to study the female members of his audience, an exercise that he had begun upon arrival at the White House. He was in search of choice meat. And, there it was before his very eyes, in various shapes and sizes. Now, if only he could manage to have one piece... For now, he resumed his glorious treatise which was fit to be perused by the most knowledgeable gymnasts of the language from which he derived his name, but which offered no meaning to the audience before him. Indeed, it was the mystery of his declamation, the incomprehensibility of his words, that fascinated *him*, the speechifier, that gave him the urge to give more to those people astonished by his shallow intelligence.

"Our dear President recognizes the impossibility of unknotting the

157

umbilical cord that attaches together all the blacks of the universe. Therefore, he would like you to join him in planning the destiny of universal Man in this auspicious moment of our unalloyed glory."

King and his people could not believe their ears, naturally. A legendary chimpanzee making such a speech. Black English excelling in whitey's society. It would, after all, be profitable to establish and maintain close relationship with those people. They would help the brothers and sisters in Blamerica to beat whitey at his own game. That thought, innocent and sincere as it was, really touched the roots of the Race's history: Images of black foster-children mesmerizing white gentlemen in the latter's House of Parliament with words of wisdom, with a language extolling love, with the hope of eternal harmony for humanity. Images of black presidents pulverizing their people with the poison of the pen later translated into a policy of prostitution. Images of black and white hypocrites hugging one another while haggling over the fate of nations existing in name only. They make the speeches, they believe not what they say, except in their sleep with their harlots in hidden hotels.

Agreement was reached to entertain the august visitors for the night. They would depart on the following day. Fineface was overwhelmed with joy. His head, usually saturated with grammar, was stuffed with feminine figures. He certainly needed some relaxation. His choice had been made, at last.

She was a svelte, chestnut-colored beauty with the face of a Madonna, the look of a day in spring, and the body of a new-born baby. His hawkish eyes were stuck on her at the end of his speech, and they remained so while he and she were together in that room. He wasted no time in making his choice known to King himself. He politely whispered it to the latter's ear as after-lunch drinks were being served. King asked to be shown the specific body in question. The admirer obliged. The host threw his head back and burst into a boisterous laughter. No problem at all, not in the least. The object of Fineface's desire would be his hostess for the night.

The rest of the day was spent doing nothing besides talk. That was to be expected, because the task ahead required long, well-laid plans. Black folk, everybody agreed, could not afford to bungle things as whites had done.

The conversation, after drifting from women, to women, and back to women, came to the white question. The Blafrican president had instructed his men to return home with white slaves, at all costs. Fineface had been perplexed by the situation at the airport, where blacks, and a few white women, were all he saw. He had thought that, possibly, the white men, all of them, were on vacation.

The hosts and their guests agreed that white male absence could not be condoned during their race's one-week reign. Yet, no one had any suggestion as to how to ferret out the absentee masters. One Blafrican who, until then, had said nothing, found his lost tongue, and suggested that the delegation consult the oracle upon their return home. He said that his grandfather, a traditional priest, had left him a few items of the profession, and that he always relied on them as a last resort. In the meantime, as a last resort in Blamerica, they would simply have to wait and see.

At dusk, Fineface and his oracle colleague took a walk outside the White House. The former did it out of boredom and impatience. He had been drinking himself silly in the company of his colleagues and a few of their hosts. What was a glass of wine without a woman? It was like a body without a heart! Only heaven knew who on earth gave those jelly-bodied women the permission to leave the room. They were expected back for a meeting with their men later that night, but Fineface was tired of begging the slow clock to move faster. For his part, his colleague, Mr. Babalawo, was yearning to see the people, to study them, and possibly to take a few of them back home to Blafrica. He had cherished the hope of obtaining some white bodies -the ideal sacrifice to the god of wealth!- but black ones, too, would be acceptable. Both would fulfill the necessary conditionality! After all, they belonged to the richest nation in the universe.

He remembered some of the stories that Mr. President himself used to tell his cabinet members in his light-hearted moments: In Blamerica, money practically flew out of the mint into people's pockets. You did not have to work hard to attain wealth; all you needed was guile, or guns. Cunning was contagious. Guile was a common quality.

And Mr. President was a truthful liar. True to the nature of his kind. True to the principle of his type. Life itself is a lie. You have got to do everything you can, to get by, and over. Blamerica, land of liars. Blamerica, lair of lions. Where parents charge their offspring for board and lodge, even when the latter have to borrow to pay up. Where brother takes his twin to court for a freak accident that occurred in the latter's courtyard. Where wife sues husband hours after the wedding bells stop ringing, because she is fed up and wants a divorce, with a cool million for her troubles. Where, in essence, man means money.

Fineface and Babalawo did not walk too far, for fear of being lost in the long streets full of people pushing and shoving one another on their journey to the house of wealth. "Now, why were they in so much hurry?" the Blafricans wondered. Did they not understand their position as controllers of the global village, and designers of universal destiny? Their rush reminded the Blafricans of their own capital in the colonial era, when those crazy colonialists never gave the black man a chance to take life as it should be taken: EASY. The few still guilty of such manners, neo-colonialist stooges, would have to be banned from Blafrican streets!

Babalawo was still studying faces, and trying to read people's minds. Only, like a man grabbing at a drop of water in a vast ocean, he could not catch a face, or a mind. Moreover, those black and brown faces appeared to be all teeth, the way they never stopped laughing. He wondered whether any of them had the serious disposition necessary for a strong foundation of wealth. Perhaps he should be contented after all with his Blafrican sacrificial lambs. Perhaps the white men would return.

The two visitors returned to the White House just in time for dinner, served at the Blafrican hour, that is, rather late at night. Fineface did not eat. He complained of stomach trouble, and asked to be excused. King cracked a joke about stomach-aches being symptomatic of heart-aches, and all those present laughed hilariously, to the embarrassment of the heart patient. Fineface was shown to his room, so that he could rest. On his way out, he whispered to King not to forget that he urgently needed a female nurse, precisely his choice of the afternoon, to take care of his many aches. King nodded in apparent agreement.

King still found it difficult to understand those people. Did they not have women in their country? Were they not there in Blamerica to do a job, the magnitude of which should leave no room for trite subjects such as women? And, who gave that man the impression that he could take a woman from Blamerica?

King called one of his aides, and told him to arrange for some women to entertain their guests while they were having after-dinner drinks. Before you could say, "hallelujah," the whole room was echoing with soulful rhythms of a quality good enough to make angels break into an uplifting boogie. Caliban Mason-Dixon King, president of Blamerica for one week, outdid everybody else. He was an angel on the floor. He picked a well endowed beauty from the array of colorful bodies in attendance, and got down to it. He had the flexible body of a gymnast, the agile feet of a sprinter, and the cadenced movement of a computerized automaton.

"Shu nuff, baby, the Good Lawd gave nigger some rhythm!"

"Eh, see how de man be jumping up and down like an antelope. Me, I dare not try dat. I can't come and break my neck-o."

"Dem Blafricans ain't seen nothin' yet; let them wait till the brothas and sistahs back in the Den got to doin' their thang. Pity they'be back home by then."

Fineface English Oniya was actually back home in his sleep, dreaming of himself as the new president of Blafrica. He woke up just when he was about to make his inaugural speech to the nation. He moved his hands all over the giant bed. No sign of human presence, no scent of a female body. He groped for the switch, pressed the button, reached for his clothes, dressed, and left the room.

The crowd in the reception room was at the height of joyful fever. There was King himself, the cynosure of all eyes, a dolphin performing in an aquarium. His dancing partner looked familiar to Fineface. He rubbed his eyes, to be sure that he was seeing right. He stumbled towards the table where his men were seated. Babalawo came to meet him, and shouted at the top of his voice:

"You have missed a lot, I tell you, you have been missing a lot."

Fineface hardly heard the words. He walked past the table, and went to the dance-floor. He was almost knocked over by flying elbows and arms, and by feet kicking as high as the ceiling. After what to him was more than an hour, he reached King's side. He did not mean to interrupt his dance, he did not mean to be rude, he merely wished to tell his host to release his chosen nurse to come rid his tortured body of overwhelming aches.

Everything happened in a flash. Fineface was knocked cold. His compatriots knelt by his side, holding his heavy head. King stood over them, his Good Book in hand, the chestnut beauty clinging to him like a slave about to be snatched from her resisting mother. Poor Fineface was suffering from ailments far worse than stomach and heart aches. He had concussion, broken ribs, and a fractured arm. Brotherhood and diplomatic decorum dictated that he be given the best treatment available. King, still clinging to the Good Book while his chestnut beauty clung to him, walked sadly to the phone, and called for one of the resident doctors. A difficult procedure, at first; but one finally arrived, a very dark one, who had Fineface taken to the hospital.

❁　❁　❁

President Robinson Immanuel Prospero was pacing back and forth in his glass room. He was worried. He had been ever since he sent out his emissaries. Already, two days were gone from the week of glory, and nothing concrete had been accomplished. Or, almost nothing: At least, he had encouraged his people to be human and productive. He had instituted an eight-day week. He had created for them a life of luxury. He was well aware that a great deal still had to be done, and he was resolved to do it. The Master would be so impressed with his achievement that He would decide to make the black arrangement permanent!

Now, if only his men could return to Blafrica with white slaves. The notion would not stop gnawing at his ulcerous interior. He was fidgety and irritated by almost everything; he could not even sleep with his new wife! The intercontinental communications system, officially commissioned by him three months before, had broken down. It was therefore impossible to phone the men in Blamerica, Blantilla, or elsewhere.

A muffled knock on the door.

"Yeeeeeees, come in, if you must!"

It was the bull-dog of a servant there to announce the birth of Mr. President's latest offspring.

"A boy? A boy, hein? Tell me, you bastard, is it a boooooooy?!!!"

The poor bastard very much aware of his parents' identity, knew nothing about the child's gender. He had simply been asked by one woman to give master the good news about the new baby.

Mr. President, in an attempt to run over the burly figure barring his way, bounced off him like a rubber-ball, and fell flat on his face. Luckily for him, his glasses remained in one piece. The bull-dog helped him to his feet. Mr. President ran out, swearing to send the bull-dog's prostitute of a mother as sacrifice to the devil.

He did not have far to go to hear the full news. An aide met him at the porch: His new baby was a girl, again! More news arrived before he could digest the bitter pill of the birth. The aide announced the return of the delegations to Boomland and Queensland. Both had interesting stories to tell. A meeting was scheduled for midnight.

Mr. President was at his wit's end. Perhaps it was time to try a woman from another land. A white woman, possibly? He should have given his men an order to bring one back specifically for the purpose of producing a baby-boy. Well, it was not too late; not yet...

Damn you! Why are you alluding to my sister again? I have told you over and over again, she is out of your reach... You say what? Of course, she is not sterile; she is as productive as they come, she has even given me a bouncing baby-boy! Oh, no! What did I just say? I didn't mean that, I'm awfully sorry. A big joke, I can assure you. How the hell could I be sleeping with my own sister? Come on, and she is actually a virgin! As innocent as a prostitute, you know what I mean? All right, you want the story of your poor, lousy brother recounted in the public arena? But, I thought you'd told them already. No way, they won't hear that from me! They know, or they should know, that your brother was a protégé of Mr. President's; that the latter sent him to National University where he obtained his degree in Political Science. Your brother was his mentor's messenger, and he used to spend the better part of his time in the air. Remember the nickname you yourself gave him? The Black Bird of Blafrica. The Black Bird carried bundles of cash to foreign banks on behalf of his mentor who, as you and I know, was saving the money for the people. Now, put yourself in the man's shoes; what would you have done if your messenger had tried to carry your message to the wrong man? Don't be mad now, just be fair, and objective. Well, your brother went to jail, not as an intellectual, but because he was trying to steal from a thief. You do realize that the patriotic thing to do, is to steal from the innocent who won't give you any problem at all. Give your brother that message from me when next you visit him in his cell. And, watch it now, don't go deliver the message to the wrong man!

Mr. President met his emissaries at midnight, and heard the report on their glorious trips. The plane carrying the delegation to Queensland had been unable to land due to bad weather. It was diverted to an airport in a country inhabited by yellow-skinned people who spoke a language as strange as their skin. It was mutually agreed -silence and action spoke louder than words- that the Blafrican intruders should leave at once. That is why they returned home to refuel and report their adventure, before taking off again for their original destination.

Mr. President told them to forget the trip. The gentlemen sent to Boomland arrived there safe and sound, only to find a lily-white society. They were fortunate that their hosts spoke English. The latter politely advised them to return home as quickly as possible, if they did not wish to be forcibly put to work in the mines.

No news from Blantilla yet. None from Blamerica either.

❖   ❖   ❖

Back in the prisons, the intellectuals were planning their strategy. A tract, composed by none other than Booker W. Kongo, the president's self-proclaimed classmate, was smuggled out to *National Guardian*, the only newspaper in the capital. It demanded the President's resignation for incompetence, inhumanity, and insensitivity. According to Mr. Kongo, Blafrica could do far better with the Master's gift than to set up a series of ill-advised, barbaric processes and objectives. The President was called a *blackassed blunderer trying to build a nation on bunkum*. He was guilty of decadence and degeneracy, etc., etc., etc. Once Mr. Kongo was given the chance to replace him, the nation would surely be set on a straight course to heaven here on earth.

I remember you read that tract, too, and you laughed like a fool. You half-educated men! You descendants of the biblical Thomas! You never appreciate the good things of life. Mr. Kongo's paper proved that he was a genius, no more, no less. He made me use my dust-covered dictionary and I really appreciate that in any man. You say his empty talk laid down no program to match Mr. President's. Well, what do you want? The man made a promise to lead us to heaven, so what could match that? Huh! You can never please people. You just criticize everybody and everything. And, don t dare start again on my sweet sister!!!

So, the tract appeared in the newspaper in the morning, and the editor disappeared in the afternoon. The coincidence was, indeed, remarkable. The poor fellow must have been fed up with life. He must have been seeking a moment like that, to cause sensation, to raise questions in people's minds. For, no one dared think that the revered Mr. President would have a hand in a nonentity's French leave. At a time of national glory, with the great task in hand, the great Mr. President could not be bothered with such trifling matters.

If only they would bring news about the white slaves. Robinson Immanuel Prospero stood on the balcony of his mansion. The city was enveloped in darkness. The lights were out everywhere, including his palace. Thank God for candles. Time, he thought, was running out on the Race. Candles... *If only the white slaves would arrive...* Candles... So much depended upon them... He had everything worked out in his mind. Blafrica would show the Master what a glorious race blacks constituted. She would prove once and for all that man's destiny should have been controlled by blacks from creation day. *If only the white slaves were there!*

But they never came. In their place came a mob led by Booker W. Kongo, Mr. President's classmate whom the latter had never seen before in his life. *Now, there you go again bothering me about details. The public knows all these things, and yet you keep insisting that we tell them. I hate repetition. Reminders are necessary, you say? I guess I agree with you there. Once in a while, we all tend to forget facts that should be forever present in our minds. If not, how do we explain the rash of repeated errors, the obstinacy of foolishness, the obduracy of beastliness in people who are supposedly human? Like the President having all those female children. Like you always thinking of my sweet sister. Like blacks believing in the Master.*

The disappearance of the editor of *National Guardian* shocked many people, not because it was unusual to hear of such events, but because the cadaver of any missing man was usually seen hours later floating in a river, squeezed into a dustbin, or gracing the corner of some alley, or some prominent crossroads. When no news was heard about the poor editor, the normal inhabitants of the nation's prisons, the criminal and the crass, the devilish and the downtrodden, began to raise their voices in protest. The intellectuals were not overtly bothered about the editor's fate -intellectuals hardly welcome journalists into their ivory tower-, but seized the opportunity to voice their grievances, and to get out of jail. In the central prison where the President's classmate was staying, total chaos would have set in, had the man not taken control of the situation. Arguments were rising to a dangerous level. One group sought immediate information on the editor's body, because the dead must be buried. Another wanted to put the question directly to Mr. President. Yet another argued that the editor deserved to be publicly executed, not dragged away in the dark. By using the latter action, the necessary lesson was lost on the population. The intellectuals doggedly emphasized Mr. President's collusion in the covert action, and sought redress against his innumerable tyrannical acts. With Mr. Booker W. Kongo and his big, bookish brain, and the nonentities' credulous demeanor, the anarchical objective was soon achieved.

But not without a little difficulty, in the persons of the prison-warders. Devoted representatives of Mr. President, dedicated servants of the State, devout adherents to the principle of justice for all, those men in uniform were ready to sacrifice their lives and souls, in order to make the prisoners remain in custody where they belonged. Mr. President himself had promised them heaven on our hellish earth if, particularly, they kept the intellectuals behind bars. The Chief Warder of our great nation was stationed in Central Prison, and it was to him that Booker W. Kongo personally appealed. The man was enraged at the very suggestion that he desert his great leader, especially at that moment of national, racial, and universal import. He was foaming at the mouth with anger, and also due to a lingering epileptic condition. He swore that Booker W. Kongo and those like him, would rot in jail as long as he was in charge of prisons. He even rushed at his remarkably calm quarry, apparently in an attempt to hit him. A stroke of fortune for all concerned: Only the man's polluted saliva hit its target, the blow having been planted on the face of a uniformed peacemaker.

Booker W. Kongo had the magic words, and he finally used them:

"Well, dear, distinguished brother, since you refuse to partake of the patriotic cake and to join forces with the well-meaning, quintessentially nationalistic elements of this great nation, I shall offer your portfolio in the new government to a more accommodating individual. And..."

Mr. Chief Warder did not allow him to conclude. His face was aglow with the eternal light of imminent luxury, his head was filled with pictures of big things of superficial quality which he had believed unattainable in his lifetime. He literally pushed one of his men, the one whom he had accidentally punched on the face, toward the gate.

However, the poor fellow did not have the keys; they were locked away in the Chief's office, as usual. The Chief stumbled out breathlessly to fetch them.

The prisoners were all given their freedom.

At the presidential palace, Robinson Immanuel Prospero was squinting behind his thick lenses. The approaching figures were carrying torches and, for one split second, his mind went back to stories that he had heard in his student days, of white hordes burning black homes in Blamerica. Maybe, indeed, the whites had come; he would welcome them in any form, in any role. The voice of Booker White Kongo, with a thick national accent, erased all notions of white presence from Mr. President's mind.

Mr. President made for his glass room. As he began to move, his glasses fell off his face and landed in the midst of the advancing men. A wretched-looking prisoner snatched them and put them on his haggard face.

In his glass room, Mr. President stood before his mirrors and saw strange images. A gorgon's head placed on triple necks. Tentacular limbs protruding from overlapping bodies of indefinable forms. He must be getting out of his mind! He, the most level-headed, clear-sighted person in the nation. He, the most handsome, happy President that Blafrica ever had. He... He must be running mad!!! He walked stealthily towards the mirrors one more time, scared of his one great love of admiring himself. He started smashing everything to pieces, but the more he smashed, the larger the gorgon's head seemed to grow.

Outside, Booker White Kongo and his men were undecided, suddenly. It was only after seeing the President that the real implication of an ouster dawned upon them. What if the Master was against a change of leadership during that week of glory? How would the new regime spend the last four days? What would they do with Robinson Immanuel Prospero himself?

So, you say those are banal questions that would interest only foolish people? Maybe our intellectuals are fools. Aren't we all? Learned fools and unlearned fools, take your pick. Cultured crooks and crude crooks, you may have your say. I would rather be the former, though. Well, don't stand there and point an accusing finger at me, when you yourself are worse. Remember how you got your university job? Your uncle the great politician saw the vice-chancellor at a party organized for one of the latter's girlfriends, to help her properly celebrate the birthday of his own deceased girlfriend, and your sinecure was offered to you because the vice-chancellor's lady told the politician that she liked your dancing. And, yes, I do recall my own saga at the university. I licked the boots of every professor whose profession was politics, until one of them, never one to be contented with a little show of gratitude, tried to put me down in the presence of my wife. Of course, you remember that I gave the senile idiot a dirty slap, and resigned my appointment with immediate effect. Then, my wife left me for being rude to a superior officer, and moved in with my victim as punishment for my foolishness. So, I have been drifting ever since. So, I still go into prof's house to sleep with my wife. So, what? All that is not relevant to our black story, or is it? Black Gods, we all know, roll in black deeds. A black President of a black people. Black buffoons posturing as politicians, and patriots, and presidents. Black intellectuals with black intelligence. Blafrica. Blamerica. All black, and dark, according to the decision of the civilized, and you know that the Master is white, and the first civilized citizen of the universe.

❊   ❊   ❊

Fineface English Oniya was recuperating rather quickly from his wounds, thanks to the efficient doctors and the concerned, competent nurses. It was so much unlike what he was used to.

Caliban Mason-Dixon King could not visit him, naturally, because state matters took up his precious time. The specific matter of that hour concerned the choice of a wife. The President of such a great nation should be responsible. To be responsible, is to take a wife even when there are a million other wenches in the shadows. To be responsible, is to be happily married forever even when husband and wife have been happily separated for as long as they have been married. To be responsible, is to have an image, to portray an illusion, to live lies. King wanted the chestnut beauty for himself, but did not want to offend his guest; he therefore took time debating with himself whether to choose another woman, or to let the love-struck guest leave before solemnizing his wedding. The second option was best for the nation, he thought.

Meanwhile, the ad hoc committee running the nation had decided to send a delegation to Blafrica with the departing guests. They would fly back in time to fully implement any plan before the Master's one-week gift expired. The time was short, but they knew full well that, in life, the best things are done in the shortest time. Like building a castle in Spain in one's dream. Like becoming a millionaire by one swift, secret action. Like blacks becoming masters of the universe through the Master's mysterious message.

Fineface, it was decided by the attending doctors, could go home the following day. He was at once downcast and elated. The picture of his chestnut beauty had remained glued to his brain, and he could not stop thinking of what might have been. However, he was gladdened by the thought of returning home. Home. The wine. The women. One of the last visitors to his hospital bed was his oracle compatriot, Mr. Babalawo.

"Mr. Fineface," said the maker of money, "you cannot come and die because of a woman, you know. We are so many miles away from home, and you know what our dear President sent us here to do. Besides, I personally don't see anything special in these women here. They are not worth a brass farthing when you really think of it. But, if you cannot get this thing out of your mind, I think we can do something. You will see, we can do something."

Babalawo was as mysterious as his name indicates. He did not even allow Fineface to ask questions before he left the room, smiling and shaking his oblong head. They were due to fly back home the following afternoon, and preparations had to be made.

Fineface English Oniya barely slept that night.

Caliban Mason-Dixon King could not sleep either, but for another reason: the continued absence of white people in his domain.

Early the next morning, the patient was conveyed back to the White House. He was like a mummy swathed as he was in bandages. He was in good spirits, nonetheless. Babalawo was waiting for him. The words of the previous night were still echoing in Fineface's mind: *We can do something...* And, they did do something.

King had left a message for Fineface to see him upon arrival at the White House. The Blamerican President was in his study when the patient entered. King was, indeed, sorry for him, with his body resembling a white balloon. Their conversation, mostly marked by silence, did not last but a few minutes. Their encounter had helped them both

169

cultivate some respect for each other. The respect could be equated to repressed desire to murder. It was the respect of two diametrically opposed brothers talking of love but thinking hate. They both smiled knowingly, two accomplices in a war which extended far beyond their dark skins. They both knew that, just as north and south never could come together, it was inconceivable that brothers separated by vast oceans of ideas and attitudes, would reach out and touch each other's soul. And their eyes, expressions of apparent calm, participated in their game of falsehood. Dreams turning into nightmare. Laughter hiding tears. So, in the jungle of civilized Blamerica, brother shook hands with brother, with the mutual hope that the other would disappear forever, or degenerate to the level of an animal. In the elevated mind of the hypocritical King, Fineface was only good for his savage land, part of the fauna of an ex-fatherland best forgotten. In the perverted soul of the benevolent Fineface, King was a mere second-class citizen subbing for the real saviors of his society. Perhaps both men would never meet again, but they had eternally marked each other. Precisely, they and their Race had been branded indelibly.

King informed Fineface that the Blamerican delegation was ready to accompany the Blafricans back to their country. The oral message to Mr. President of Blafrica was, that he should try to do without the services of white slaves, because blacks ought not to repeat the beastly acts perpetrated by whites and, more importantly, an essential aspect of black liberation was the necessity for blacks to do things for themselves, to prove that they, too, were achievers.

In King's mind, even as he was talking to his departing abhorred brother, thoughts of the absentee whites prevailed. *If only they would return.* He would give anything to see them emerge from wherever they were; he would even give up plans to marry his chestnut beauty.

The departure of the Blafrican and Blamerican representatives was a moving scene, fit for the most dramatic civilized theatre. It was high noon. In spite of his wounds, Fineface hugged and kept hugging his brothers and sisters. With each hug, he shuddered with pain, and cursed under his breath, while his face was radiant with joy. His colleagues were too busy carrying into the aircraft all sorts of gifts for friends, family, and selves, to participate in the emotional leave-taking. For their part, the accompanying delegation from Blamerica left their people reluctantly. Some tears were shed here and there, amid mumblings of premonition of death. On the whole, one could rightly say that the men were imbued with patriotic fervor; they were going on a mission clearly essential to the grandeur of Race and Nation, and that was enough to gratify their hearts. They were well prepared for the journey. They had every item needed to exist abroad: water, food, clothes, drinks, a limousine, gas, women, mobile homes, and bottled air...

Babalawo was nowhere to be found. Fineface noticed his absence just as he was boarding the plane. To his surprise, his compatriot was already quite settled inside. Beside him sat the chestnut beauty. Indeed, they had done something!

⊕   ⊕   ⊕

Back on the ground, King was seething with anger. The news of the chestnut beauty's disappearance reached him hours after the plane had taken off. He had it all worked out, or so he thought: That very night, he was going to announce his engagement in the presence of his united people; for, a very reliable source had made it known that the white men were coming back after all. His wife and the white men would alter the course of his life and, invariably, that of the entire nation. It turned out to be an empty dream, unfortunately. The very reliable source who had sworn to the return of the whites, also gave Mr. President the news of his beauty's absence. And well he should know, since it was he, one of the President's most faithful, most trustworthy disciples, who had helped Babalawo smuggle the willing woman into the plane.

Caliban Mason-Dixon King was dejected. He was desolate. He was desperate. That was the last straw, as far as he was concerned. After all the kindness he had shown in his few days in the White House. After all the hospitality he had shown those barbaric brothers. After all the plans he had made for building bridges across racial and sexual lines, for establishing true Christianity in his nation, for making Blamerica a nation safe for children and women. How could life be so cruel to him? He was definitely too good for this world. The sinners simply had to be punished by extermination, because they had no right to pollute the world, his world, with their presence.

He recalled hearing several times on his television that the White House was equipped with a button that, with a simple push, would set off a device capable of destroying the whole world, except the White House itself. The idea fascinated him. He had with him possible constituent elements for creating a new world, almost. *If only the white men would return...*

He ran to the presidential study, and did not have long to search. There it was, a white button, hardly visible, with one word boldly marked beside it: DANGER.

He was never afraid of danger. He had lived with it, lived through it, lived it, all his life. Images of unsheathed knives and corked guns in the dark. Images of starved dogs dangerously close to being released from a loose leash. Images of a yawning abyss with a care-free, black boy teetering on the slippery edge. And the image of a chestnut beauty being raped by a full-fanged black man!

King held his breath and pressed the white button. What happened was totally unexpected.

❖   ❖   ❖

So, you are still insisting that I would do best to leave this dear nation of ours. And, I refuse to budge an inch. You see, I am the pus-hosting thumb of your infected right hand; you cannot cut me off. I am the alienated first wife of your harem of harlots; you cannot cut off the cord. I am your image in the mirror; you cannot blot me out. I am your prodigal son newly returned from a sojourn of suffering in a heaven of hatred; you cannot deny me. At least, I made it back home. Remember that many others did not, do not, and never will. Like Fineface, and Babalawo, and the black brothers and sisters from Blamerica. Like you and your imported existence. Like you and your borrowed life. Like you and your adulterated existence which is nothing but nonsense.

Well, let me finish the story before you and I try to settle down to drinking the dregs left by those whom we know but refuse to know. The intellectuals, and I heard you say you were not one of them, the intellectuals and their obedient servants trooped undisturbed into the presidential palace to find the man in his glass room, lying there without any sign of life.

The intellectuals feared the worst, but hoped the worst had happened. Booker White Kongo ordered everyone out of the building. He

172

told them to go home and pray for the quick recovery of the fallen man. They left reluctantly. Booker White stayed behind and planned to be there permanently. He would move in his family and start at once to work for the good of his people. The remaining couple of days of the Master's extraordinary gift did not really matter to him because, after all, only a fool would prefer a provisional supremacy to a lifetime rule. To be sure of that absolute, eternal power, he himself looked into the glass room where Mr. President, precisely, ex-President, lay prostate.

The lights were soon restored, to Booker's annoyance. It was as if the lights revealed some monstrosities that he had committed. Yet he had no reason on earth to be ashamed, or to hide.

While Mr. Booker White Kongo, presidential candidate turned self-appointed president, was contemplating his newly won domain, the Square, rather quiet since the announcement of the Master's message to the Blacks, was filling up with the night people. Feet moving from nowhere to no destination. Bodies floating about aimlessly like a kite carried by the wind. Minds filled with ideas as precise as the unknown number of President Prospero's children.

You say that those people had a purpose for being at the Square, but I do not agree with you, to a certain extent. Maybe some mysterious power drew them to that spot that very night. Maybe their minds, as collective as the communal culture which had given birth to their selfish personalities, spoke to one another on the phone-line as functional as Blafrica's unanswered prayers to God. Yes, I would buy that possibility, especially because our lines never work, perfect symbols of our culture of decoration. For whatever reason, those people were flocking to the Square after their brief holiday. Then, out of nowhere appeared the figure, familiar to us all, in his shining three-piece suit, and holding a gold-colored Bible.

There you go again, disagreeing with me for no reason at all. Why, for heaven's sake, why? Well, maybe the man had descended directly from heaven, which would be perfectly all right. We all know that our nation is full of Jehovahs and Jesuses, self-appointed and unexpected, here to save our irretrievably condemned people. Maybe the man came from the presidential palace; he could be the President himself, for all you and I know. Maybe it was even you!!! Just think of all the possibilities, how interesting they would be, how true they are, what fantastic lies they constitute, for our dear nation.

Now, on this point we agree: The man in the shining suit was the Master's messenger. But, perhaps, we are wrong. How about that? Perhaps he was a true messiah. Or, Caliban Mason-Dixon King. Or, a drifter from somewhere. Anyway, he looked fatter than before. He looked lighter in complexion, and happier, too. Unlike the first time, he said not a single word. He just stood there, staring at the continuously increasing crowd which had unconsciously formed a circle around him.

I don't exactly recollect how it happened, but people began to point accusing fingers at the strange man. It was, as I heard you exclaim, impossible! People at the Square were never known to accuse anyone of anything. Perfect followers of leaders of all shapes, and colors, they had been known to proclaim a beggar God; to glorify a pimp; to worship a bull-dog; even to lick the boots of a madman, for no other reason than their God-given humanism.

But there they were, threatening the man in the shining suit. *Remember, I told you not to join in that nasty act, but you refused to listen. It is now that I know why you did not. Yes, you lousy man, my sister never stopped attracting you, did she? And you always wanted to impress her. Let me tell you the one and only truth. It will shock you, it might even make you consider suicide and, maybe, you would be well advised to take that liberating action: My sister is not my sister; she is my woman!!! I see your heart ceasing to beat. I see the fire in your lecherous eyes beginning to dim. I see the explosive ire running through your wicked veins. Watch it, however. I am telling a lie; I just wanted to see your reaction, ah, ah.*

You were the first to throw a stone at the strange man. Today, you claim not to know what you were doing, but you did it all the same. Remember how quickly others followed suit? My sister-woman was so excited that the hook on her bra became undone, and you were only too pleased to hold her close to your heart, to keep her from being trampled to death, at least so you said. I thank you for saving her life. But, note this: If you try it again, I shall do something to you that will stop you from making passes at other people s women.

So, you and people like you started throwing stones at the man. And the wrath of the Master came down upon you all. But, I still do not understand how only the man, you, my sister-woman, and I, escaped.

The confusion was unimaginable. People were running over one another. Children and women were crying hysterically and the men, as cool as prisoners standing before a death-squad, were pissing and defecating in their pants. The cause of the pandemonium: The plane bringing back Fineface English Oniya, his colleagues, and their Blamerican guests, had made a forced landing at the Square. Again, you tell me that it was not forced to land, that the pilot, a patriot to the core, meant to land there, so as to introduce the guests directly to the people. Perhaps you are right. He certainly did an excellent job introducing blacks to one another. Joined together in death just as they had lived in harmony in life, those Blamericans and Blafricans became acquainted in a bang. Metal and men came into contact and, in harmony, resolved their conflicts in a united explosion which must have echoed in places as far away as Blantilla, Queensland, Boomland and, of course, Blamerica, the source of the whole accident. Plane and people embraced one another eternally, in a love so fiery that the flames were seen thousands of miles away.

Fineface died in the arms of his chestnut beauty, and no end could have been more appropriate to that extraordinary affair. Babalawo died in the middle of two possible sacrificial lambs to his God named Money. And, no death has been known to be so well deserved. Those people casting stones at the peaceful man in the shining suit, by passing away on that fateful night, achieved an objective that definitely set them apart from millions dreaming of touching a plane in their lifetime: Not only did they touch a plane, they died with a plane.

In the smoldering debris of men and metal, the man in the shining suit was holding up his Bible and staring at my sister. *How dare you say that she is my woman!* He stuck out his tongue, and began to lick his thick lips.

We did not have a chance to witness the man's subsequent actions because, just then, the lights went out, again! Remember, we all stuck together, hand in hand, body to body, you, my sister, and I? You said that you were afraid of the man. My sister said that she was scared of the Master, but the only person I feared was you.

Don't ask me why, because you know more than anyone else and, this time, I refuse to make any explanation. Besides, what do you want, after all? You have been saved from the holocaust. You are one of a handful who managed to escape destruction. And, don't forget that the Master has not yet taken away your great privilege.

One thing that has worried me, though, since all those strange

175

events occurred: What have you done with the Master's gift? What has become of your privilege? The President's white slaves never came. What is more interesting is, that we are not even sure of what became of our dear Mr. President himself, and of Booker White Kongo. Or, perhaps, I should say that I am aware of it, but would rather keep it a secret from you and others. That is what I call a real privilege. The privilege of a prostitute to know her customer's secrets, and not divulge them until they can be used to destroy him. The privilege of a creator deciding to make you male and my sister female. The privilege of a cultivated coxcomb basking in the sun of inhumanity and depravity, and inviting his unwary family to join his victims.

So, what happened to Mr. President and his classmate? They are in Blamerica, working hand in hand with Caliban King in the paradise of racism and exploitation, to civilize the blacks, and be enslaved -oh, no, forgive the slip of tongue, I mean to be *civilized*- by whites. Lest I forget, the white men came back at the buzz of that button pushed by Caliban Mason-Dixon King. It turned out that the Master's telephone message was a hoax, a game played by fools on fools. And, here in Blafrica? The darkness of that night, during which the man in the shining suit disappeared, prevented us from ever finding out. Nonetheless, we know that the Master exists, that He did give us that one-week gift, that He still has not taken it back from us, that we have the right to proclaim our supremacy, and to exercise our mastery over all the other races on the planet.

The only question that lingers in my mind: What did you do with your own gift? What happened to your privilege? I am aware of one thing that you cannot stop doing: Ogling my woman, or, my sister. Now, you ask what I, too, have done. I looked into the mirror, and saw the Black Gods!!!

www.ingramcontent.com/pod-product-compliance
Lightning Source LLC
Chambersburg PA
CBHW070226030726
47505CB00006B/1845

* 9 7 8 0 9 6 2 8 8 6 4 4 7 *